Willy Slater's Lane

A NOVEL BY
Mitch Wieland

Southern Methodist University Press
Dallas

This novel is a work of fiction. Names, characters, places, and incidents are either the product of the author's imagination or are used fictitiously.

Requests for permission to reproduce material from this work should be sent to:
    Rights and Permissions
    Southern Methodist University Press
    PO Box 750415
    Dallas, TX 75275-0415

Library of Congress Cataloging-in-Publication Data
Wieland, Mitch, 1961–
    Willy Slater's lane / Mitch Wieland.
       p.   cm.
    ISBN 0-87074-408-9 (cloth). — ISBN 0-87074-409-7 (paper)
    I. Title.
    PS3573.I345W54   1996
    813'.54—dc20   96-30606

Cover art and design by Barbara Whitehead

Printed in the United States of America on acid-free paper
10 9 8 7 6 5 4 3 2 1

For Cyndi,
who never wavered

I wish to thank the many teachers and friends who offered advice on the manuscript: Allen Wier, Tamas Aczel, and Ted Solotaroff in Alabama, and Harold Jaffe, Jerry Bumpus, Marsh Cassady, Jerry Hannah, Carl Mumm, Jeff Black, and Robert Dean in California. I'd also like to thank my mother, Phyllis, for putting books in my hands from the time I could walk, and my father, John, for raising me on those vivid bedtime stories about Tuscarawas County, Ohio. A special thanks, too, to Raymond and Martha Stucky, for sharing their knowledge about the real Willy Slater's Lane.

Finally, much gratitude is expressed to George Garrett for his great support and cheerful enthusiasm. He remains the most generous man in the world of letters.

Ohio, 1980

Harlan and Erban Kern were eating breakfast in the kitchen when their living room floor collapsed. The house creaked, then trembled, the rotted floorboards giving out at last. The brothers listened to their furniture crash into the basement: the Victrola and black and white Zenith, the maple china cupboard, the rolltop desk and straight-backed chairs. With several last clanks and bangs, the old farmhouse grew quiet. Harlan peered down the dark hallway.

"Must've been the floor."

Erban nodded. He concentrated on getting a runny egg yolk onto his toast.

After breakfast the brothers shuffled down the hall, Erban, as always, the slower one. They squinted side by side into the living room. Dampness seeped through the gaping mouth of splintered wood. On a narrow ledge the sofa and bookcase sat untouched.

Harlan dragged the sofa into the kitchen. He couldn't budge the bookcase. Erban removed volume after volume of the Encyclopaedia Britannica and carried the heavy books to his room.

3

He wanted to save his parents' wedding portrait, but it hung opposite the door.

Harlan spat into the basement. "We'll just close off the room."

"Can't we get that picture?" Erban asked, studying the space where the floor used to be.

"Can you fly?"

Erban shrugged. His brother always said things he didn't want to hear.

"That settles it then." Harlan jammed the door into its warped frame. He slid a crate of insulators against the bottom of the wood. "I knew those useless things were good for something."

The Kerns were both in their late fifties. Neither brother had been seen in town in years. Once a week, Harlan's wife, Elizabeth, drove the twenty miles into Sugarcreek, where she stopped at Kroger's and returned straight home. Most towns-people considered the farm an asylum for backwoods fools.

In the late afternoon, Harlan and Erban settled into their chairs on the porch. Elizabeth Kern bounced toward them in the pickup, gravel popping under the tires. The old Ford smoked out the back. Elizabeth slowed onto the rutted path and parked in the yard.

She struggled up the steps with the groceries. The color drained from her face. Her heavy body moved ponderously, as if through deep water. Erban got up to help her with the door.

"Get the paper?" Harlan asked from his chair.

Elizabeth glared. "It's still in the truck, you lazy old fool."

Harlan frowned and turned for the yard.

Holding open the screen door, Erban tried not to notice the tension hovering like a bad smell. "The living room floor went."

"What?"

"Most everything's in the basement now." He tried to smile. "We got the couch, though."

Elizabeth snorted, triggering a coughing fit. She staggered into the house. Erban let the door rap against the frame.

"You want some of this?" Harlan asked, returning with the newspaper.

Erban shook his head. He stared down the shaded tunnel of trees stretching toward Crooked Run. The new leaves, the overgrown hedge and uncut grass—everything a different shade of green. He recalled the months of snow and ice, shivering at the memory of the deep cold. Winter came as close to dying as a man could get.

The Kerns were the only people left on the narrow back road. The other families had sold their farms to the coal company and moved on. The Hermanns had bought a farm in Winfield, the Beitzals a new house in town. The Slaters had moved down to the Ohio River, near Marietta.

Around the Kern house the rolling hills were carved open, black veins of coal exposed and dug out by the mammoth shovel of the dragline. Abandoned farmhouses and their outbuildings remained, scattered here and there among the hills, nestled in the valleys. Children broke their windows, left their doors open to swing in the wind that blew through the woods at night. Ghostly now, the buildings gave themselves back to the ground.

Harlan shook the newspaper. "Says here the Amish built another restaurant on Route 39. Five hundred seats and a special parking lot for tour buses." He spat out into the yard. "Who would drive to look at a guy in a black hat and whiskers? Or women in bonnets and long dresses?"

"They can cook," Erban said.

Harlan laughed. "Maybe we should trade old Lizzy in for an Amish woman." He rapped his knuckles against Erban's knee. "We'd eat better."

Her voice boomed through the screen. "Who would eat better?"

"You're eavesdropping again," Harlan said without turning around.

Elizabeth pushed open the door and shook her wooden spoon. "You watch your mouth, Harlan Kern," she said, "or you won't eat anything at all." The door banged shut again.

"We could only wish she'd stop cooking."

"Don't push your luck," Elizabeth shouted from the kitchen.

Erban stood up. He didn't want to be in the middle of another fight. "I'm going for my walk."

Every evening before supper Erban slowly made his way down Willy Slater's Lane, past empty farmhouses and sagging barns, then turned right or left onto Crooked Run, depending on his mood. Today he turned right and followed the paved road toward the Dayton Specht farm. The land spread out in waves of newly planted corn.

Erban searched the grass, looking for insulators the power company had once used on the poles. He had a large collection at home. Though he'd scoured Crooked Run many times over the years, he still enjoyed the hunt. The thrill of finding a new one. Their shapes reminded him of small church bells, forged in glass.

Erban walked beside land his father had owned and farmed. Forty years ago, the brothers had lost their parents to a bad seal on a Mason jar. Harlan and Erban had returned from town one afternoon to find their mother and father ill. They died three days later. Doc Krantz told everyone it was the worst case of food poisoning he'd ever seen.

At the time of his death, Benjamin Kern had title to three hundred acres of rich farmland. Two barns stood on his property, full of hay and grain. Across the open fields, binders and threshers were parked like toys he'd forgotten to put away. Without their father, Harlan and Erban didn't have the ambition to farm. They had never liked it much in the first place. Instead of helping with the harvest they had often gone swimming at the rock quarry, or out for a hike in the surrounding hills.

Through their entire youth the brothers had avoided farm work as much as possible.

After a month of struggling in the barns and fields, Harlan decided to sell. That evening Erban put on his baggy suit. He walked over to Dayton Specht's farm and knocked on the screen door.

"We can't seem to do like our daddy done," he said when Dayton came to the door.

The big man stood on the other side of the screen. "Your father was a good farmer, Erban. He made all the decisions for the place. And did most of the work." Dayton pulled the napkin from his overalls. "Might take a while, but you'll learn."

"Can't." Erban spat out the word like it was a rotten piece of food. "Harlan's got an offer for you, Mr. Specht," he said, looking at his muddy boots. "All the bottomland here along the road, next to your farm."

Dayton unlatched the screen door. "Come on in, Erban. Tell me this again."

The Kern brothers sold their land to Dayton Specht, except for the ten acres around their house. Dayton paid them directly in regular installments. Each month, Harlan stuffed the crisp twenties and fifties into Mason jars and buried them under the weeds in their yard.

A coal truck shook the ground. Erban turned from the road as bits of tar pelted his back. He hated the big semi trucks. Sometimes the drivers tried to knock him into the ditch, honking their horns as if they owned the land.

Erban spotted something in the grass ahead. He increased his pace, squinting hard. It was a crumpled beer can. He turned the thing over in his spotted hands, then dropped it and continued down the road.

At the farm, Harlan dug through the junk in the shed. He held up a worn-out carburetor, studying it in his hands. It wasn't quite what he wanted. Behind him a sheet of tar paper blew off the roof. Pages of the newspaper tumbled from the porch, catching in the spokes of the combine.

For the past two hours Harlan had searched the farm, looking for something to take apart. He enjoyed discovering how things were made. Sometimes he was able to put the spare parts together, like a puzzle, but usually he could not. He always ended up with a piece left over: a bolt, a nut, something. Once, when he did manage to put an electric motor back together, it didn't work. It probably hadn't run in years.

Harlan lifted a tangle of thin black wires. In his unsteady hand, the wires imitated a nest of snakes. He sighed and dropped the bundle at his feet. He couldn't explain the restlessness sweeping over him. That edgy feeling he sometimes felt after breakfast had never once happened in the evenings. He'd watched television with Lizzy and Erban for hours, laughing until his stomach hurt. It was only tonight, with the television set gone and the long stretch of darkness before him, that the feeling overtook him.

No more Dallas, he thought sadly.

He wasn't like Erban in the least. His brother kept his nose constantly in a book, studying about some place neither of them would ever see. And why Erban hunted those stupid insulators was an absolute mystery. His brother acted as if the things were actually worth something. Nothing Erban did had ever interested Harlan for a moment, including the nights spent watching the stars.

Harlan roamed around the yard. Rusted farm equipment stood here and there in the tall grass. He drifted into the dark barn and then out again, looked once more through the shed. Never before had he hunted for work to do. When his father had been alive, Harlan had never tried to help on the farm. Now he needed something to fill the evening. He wondered if this was how a man was supposed to feel. To know, once the sun had slid down the sky and set beyond the hill, that work had been done.

With shaking hands, Harlan picked up a hammer. He examined the dull iron head. The smooth wooden handle. He turned around and looked across the yard.

Harlan walked over to the plough. He paused a moment, his free hand opening and closing, then swung the hammer as hard as he could. The shock ran the length of his arm. He swung the hammer again and sparks flew. Another strike pitted the surface of the blade. For several minutes, Harlan beat against the plough. Sweat ran down his face. He pounded the metal with glancing blows that tore his knuckles, solid shots that numbed his hand.

Harlan held the hammer poised above his head. He felt strangely hollow—like the trees he sometimes found deep in the woods. Trees that had rotted from the inside out. He took a slow breath and dropped the hammer to the ground. Whatever had been inside him was gone.

Harlan tramped to the shed and leaned through the open door. Inside the house, Elizabeth clanked things around on the stove. The woman was ruining another meal. Once again, he dug through the pile of junk.

When he reached the twin silos of the Martin farm, Erban turned around. He hunted through the weeds along the opposite side of Crooked Run. At the Specht farm, he stopped to rest. He held onto his hat as another coal truck thundered past.

Someone spoke from across the road.

"Those things'll run you over." Dayton leaned against his porch rail. "Come visit for a while."

Erban stood motionless beside the ditch.

"Don't worry. Come talk to me."

Erban looked both ways, then hurried across the road. He climbed the porch steps.

"Let's sit," Dayton said.

Erban nodded. He hadn't spoken with a neighbor for months, let alone visited his house. He took off his hat and sat down.

"I often watch you go by, Erban."

"I've been insulator hunting."

Dayton wrinkled his brow. "My father used to collect those things. He had lots of them, some colored glass, some painted porcelain. He used to have them around like decorations, lined up on the bookcase and the china cupboard, even on the window sills. My mother got so mad at him sometimes." He chuckled. "After Dad died, she wouldn't let us move even one of those insulators. Most are still down at our old house, where the Martins live now."

Dayton looked over. "I'm sure Hans would let you have as many as you want. I'll tell him you're coming."

"I'd like that."

Erban studied the sky. The setting sun colored the horizon with dusty orange. Fireflies winked over the fields. He loved this time of day, before the coming night, when the world hung on the verge of darkness.

Dayton spoke from the shadows. "Everything all right out home?"

"There's no problems." Erban pictured Harlan traipsing around the farm, tearing things apart so he could put them together. "My brother works a lot around the place."

"How's his wife?"

"She don't complain none."

Dayton rubbed his chin. "You folks have enough money?"

Erban almost mentioned the Mason jars in the yard. How there were fewer of them every year. He caught himself at the last moment. Harlan would be crazy with anger if he told.

"We've got no problems," he said.

Cora Specht opened the screen door. "Supper."

"I should go," Erban said, rising from the chair.

"Eat with us." Dayton patted him on the back. "We'd like the company."

Erban thought about his brother at the house. Elizabeth would be setting the table, ready for them to eat. Not that Harlan would wait. He ate when the food was hot, regardless of anyone else. But Harlan would be mad when he learned Erban had eaten at the Spechts. Harlan found something to yell about every day of his life.

Dayton held open the door. "Hurry, now. Cora's biscuits are best right from the oven."

Serving plates and bowls crowded the table, reminding Erban of mealtimes long past. His mother's cooking had tasted so good, every single time. He still missed his parents deeply, despite the passing years. Their memory rested in his heart as if it were part of the blood and muscle.

Cora pulled out a chair next to a platter of fried chicken. "Sit here, Erban."

Dayton and Cora bowed their heads. Erban nodded, remembering his parents had also prayed before every meal. The Spechts joined hands and reached out to him. Erban slipped their rough palms against his own. After a moment, Dayton and Cora opened their eyes.

"Hand me your plate," Cora said.

Throughout the meal, Erban found it difficult to follow what was being said. He saw his father at the table, scooping mashed potatoes from the mixing bowl. Mother reaching for his plate. They had always made sure he ate enough. Father used to say Erban would make a good scarecrow, then would look over and wink.

After dinner, Dayton leaned back in his chair. "Hans Martin heard from his boy in California," he said, sipping coffee. "He has a job out there in a machine shop."

"I don't see why he didn't stay around here." Cora stacked

empty bowls onto her plate. "That boy always had an itch in his pants. He was never happy unless he was moving."

She turned to Erban. "You knew John Martin, didn't you?"

"I remember him." The Martin boy had swept floors and emptied trash after school while the rest of the children played outside. John had been quiet and shy, and Erban had liked him for that. In school, Erban never cared for the boys who liked to shout.

"Can you picture California?" Dayton said. "I guess John swims in the ocean sometimes."

Erban had read much about the Pacific. His encyclopedias had a whole section about it. He knew the ocean's average depth and temperature, the types of life it contained. He could even recite its exact dimensions.

"Swimming in the ocean, just like the stars on television," Cora said. "It's hard to believe."

"Our television's gone," Erban said, remembering.

Dayton set down his cup. "Maybe you blew a circuit. That happened to us."

"We lost the living room floor. It broke through this morning while we were eating breakfast."

Cora turned from the sink and looked wide-eyed at her husband. "The floor collapsed?"

Erban nodded. "The spring's been running into our basement for years. The wood rotted. Harlan says the rest of the floors could go at any time." He stopped, wondering if he'd told too much.

"Why didn't you say something sooner?" Dayton asked.

"I forgot about it."

Cora wiped her hands on a towel. "It's a wonder none of you was hurt."

"We were in the other room."

"Do you need help with anything?" Dayton said. "Maybe there's something I can do?"

Erban shook his head. "Harlan says we'll just use the kitchen now for relaxing in the evenings. It'll be warmer there this winter, anyway, because of the stove." He raised his fork and started on his blueberry pie.

Harlan leaned forward, eating as if he expected the food to be snatched away. He tried to cut a piece of ham Elizabeth had fried. *Tough as harness leather,* he thought. He tore at the meat with his teeth, wondering if harness leather would taste better.

Elizabeth watched him eat. "Why don't you just stick your face down in the plate? It'd be easier."

"Maybe you forget where this comes from? Maybe you don't want to eat tonight?"

Elizabeth slapped him on the back. "I know where this food came from, Harlan Kern. From your daddy, that's who. You couldn't earn a dollar if your lazy hide depended on it."

Harlan pointed his fork at her heart. "You watch that mouth of yours, or you'll be sleeping in the barn." He stabbed into the meat. "Did you fry this all day?"

"Wrong again," she said. "Only since noon." She put down her fork. "Where's Erban got to?"

"Probably lost." He held his beer poised halfway to his mouth. "You let me worry about my brother." It wasn't like Erban to stay out after dark. He usually returned from his walk long before they ate. Harlan pictured his brother in a ditch, smashed like a car-hit possum.

An engine revved outside. Headlight beams swept across the kitchen wall. At the window, Harlan pulled back the curtains.

"Who is it?" Elizabeth asked.

Harlan raised his hand to silence her. An expensive-looking car had parked beside his truck, the chrome bumper gleaming in the porch light. He couldn't see anyone through the dark windshield.

Elizabeth pushed him from the window with her hip. "Who is it?"

Harlan pulled his suspenders over his shoulders, ignoring her. He stepped onto the porch. Two men in suits stood next to the car, smoothing their pants and jackets, straightening their ties. As they worked their way around the farm machinery, Harlan clenched his teeth. They reminded him of the encyclopedia salesman from years ago. He pressed against the door, his back flush with the wood.

Moonlight paled the gravel lane. Erban passed the silent farms on his way home, their barns and houses in silhouette, silos rising against the dark woods. He'd enjoyed his visit with the Spechts, sitting around the table after dinner, talking. He liked discussing things with people, once he got started. Harlan always marched away when his plate was empty, heading for the living room and the television set. Maybe without the shows to watch they would talk more in the evenings. Erban increased his pace down the lane. Perhaps Harlan and Elizabeth would get interested in the stars. He could teach them about the constellations, the movements of the planets. They could spend their summer evenings outside with him, exploring the sky.

Nearing his house, he slowed. Headlights bobbed in the darkness ahead, approaching fast. He squinted into the glare. *Who would visit us?* he thought. *Who would come?*

A bulky car emerged from the night, heading straight for him, stones ticking wildly off the fenders. He jumped into the ditch. The car sped down the lane, fishtailing past in a shower of loose gravel. Dust churned against his legs, his chest, smothered his breath. Erban looked back, his eyes raw. Through the dark haze, staring like the eyes of the devil himself, two red taillights faded from sight.

Elizabeth Kern awoke just before dawn. She wondered, in that dreamy peaceful way as the sleep left her, if she were perhaps somewhere else, some place far away. But then her eyes focused on the ceiling with its road map of water stains. The paint peelings hanging down.

On the other side of the bed, shoved to the very edge, Harlan lay on his back. He struggled through a raspy snore. Elizabeth frowned at him.

She pushed herself upright on the sagging mattress. Beyond the window dawn seeped into the sky, filling the room with milky light. Dark clouds massed above the wooded hill, weighted with rain.

Elizabeth moved cautiously to the dresser, mindful of where she placed her feet. The floor could collapse at any moment. She smiled at the thought of Harlan falling through. That would be fun. And the noise the bed springs would make hitting the base-ment. The old grump would scream his head off. The thought thoroughly pleased her.

She put on her robe, brushed her hair. The floorboards creaked as she turned for the door and she froze. Harlan continued to snore. Elizabeth held her breath until she was out of the room.

In the kitchen she measured out the coffee, using more than the directions called for. Harlan, the miser, ranted and raved about her wasting coffee. "A can like this should last us a month, Lizzy," he often told her. "You're just throwing it away." For a while the old fart had waked first so he could make the coffee himself. That didn't last. She would get up before the chickens to have her coffee strong. She needed fortification for the day ahead. If she drank a few cups before Harlan awoke, her day had its proper cushion. A buffer against the thousand aggravations to come.

She stood at the sink, watching the percolator, the coffee bubbling through the glass ball on top with a pleasing sound. The room grew dark as rain clouds pushed overhead. Fat drops pattered against the pane. Even on rainy mornings like this she enjoyed looking out, past the weeds and junk in the yard, to the hills covered with trees. She opened the window a crack. The air was damp and full of the scent of blossoms.

Elizabeth had grown up in a steel mill town near the Pennsylvania border. The smokestacks turned everything iron-gray. The people never smiled. Even the houses were the color of ash. That first day, as Harlan had brought her home in the truck, Elizabeth dared to hope. Amish farms with their white houses and lush fields slid past her window. The view looked like a calendar scene from her father's diner. She opened the vent, breathed deeply. Perhaps she'd made the right move after all. Her father had thought she'd gone mad—putting an ad in the classifieds, shopping for a husband as he had so bluntly put it.

Harlan had picked her up at the bus station in Dover. In his wrinkled suit and slicked-back hair, he looked as anxious as a man meeting the President. She knew it was him right away. But Elizabeth had liked the fact he was nervous. His apprehension made her feel important, as if she were special. For a few precious moments she felt like a queen. Then, without a word, Harlan threw her two suitcases into the truck and climbed in.

She had been crazy to write the newspapers—she knew that now. But at thirty-seven, Elizabeth had given up hope of finding a husband. During high school, while her friends went out, she'd spent every Friday and Saturday night waitressing at the diner. In her entire adult life there had been only a handful of dates. None of the men—sullen workers from the local mills, their skin so gritty it would never wash clean—had asked her out again.

And what of the dates themselves? They were always the same. The men bought hamburgers at the Burger King, then drove straight to Norton's Drive-In Theater. As soon as the movie started they reached for her, pawing her breasts, groping between her legs. But she was strong. She'd learned how to cool them off.

On her last date, a stocky bastard named George Warshawski wouldn't slow down. Mad, she grabbed the bulge in his pants, squeezing and twisting as hard as she could.

"Cunt," he yelled through clenched teeth. He twisted in the seat and a white light crackled through her head. She found herself against the cold door, both of her lips split. His weight moved onto her, hard knees pressing ribs, forcing out air. The window crank jabbed her spine. She waited for the sound of her dress tearing, but instead his hands gripped her throat. Blackness edged around her eyes.

Mute terror rose from within. Before she could think she flattened his nose with her palm. Using both arms she pulled back his hand and bit until her teeth struck bone. She jerked open the door and left him whimpering on the seat.

Her first impression of Harlan Kern, however, had been greatly off the mark. What she had taken for nervousness was only a general dislike the man had for people. A hatred of everything outside his ramshackle house. He had a mean streak as long as anyone she'd ever met, her father included. When they arrived at the farm that first day, her heart fell. The house looked like something ready to be torn down. Harlan parked in the yard and turned to her.

"Come on," he'd said.

Elizabeth stared into the rain. She had traded one dreary existence for another. *At least I'm out of that dirty town,* she thought, *away from those god-awful mills.* She had seen the last of the soot and the smoke, and that was almost worth Harlan's cantankerous ways. She'd have given anything to get away from her father and his constant shouting. A trade-off. A simple shuffling of the cards in her hand.

Elizabeth sighed. Her heart swelled for no reason she could think of. Maybe it was the sight of the trees, buffeted by the wind. Or perhaps it was the dark mist, obscuring the upper half of the hill. The rain against the roof gave the kitchen a cozy feel. The farm felt as much like a home as she could hope to find.

Of course, she thought, turning from the window. How could she not have remembered? Roger Bundt, president of Copperhead Coal, standing in *their* yard last night. She pictured the brief meeting: Harlan on the porch, moths swarming the bulb over his head, Bundt in the shadows next to the plough. From what she could hear from inside the house, Bundt wanted to strip the whole way to the ravine north of the barn. He had offered to buy the entire farm, plus additional money to help them relocate. It was almost too good to be true. Now she could live in a nicer place and remain surrounded by the farmland she loved.

She paced the kitchen, halted mid-stride. *The Murphy place. The frigging Murphy place.* The farm on Crooked Run had been for sale since Lyle Murphy's heart attack last winter. Elizabeth had always admired the farmhouse on her drives into Sugarcreek, never once considering the place could be hers. Surely Harlan wasn't serious about staying in a house without a living room. He had probably turned down Bundt to get more money. Harlan knew how to get what he wanted.

Behind her the floor creaked. Erban stood in the doorway, the flap of his overalls hanging down. He rubbed at his eyes with both fists.

"Harlan still in bed?"

She smiled. He said the same thing every morning. "Do you want some coffee, Erban?" She poured two cups and set them on the kitchen table.

At the window, Erban watched the rain. "It's really coming down."

"Could rain all day." She pulled out a chair. "Come have a seat with me."

Elizabeth brought over a plate of powdered donuts and sat next to him. She liked being with Erban, though he never said much. He usually studied the table while they talked. Recently, she had caught herself looking forward to their hesitant chats. Her spirits dropped when Harlan stomped into the kitchen, yawning with that dark cavernous mouth.

"Think we'll get a new TV?" she asked, licking powdered sugar off a donut. She imagined watching color television in the living room of the Murphy place.

Erban gave the question serious thought. He pondered every question she asked him, as if the world depended on him giving the correct answer.

"I don't think Harlan wants to spend the money. He says they're all made in Japan anyway."

"But what will we do this winter?"

"Maybe we could get a radio?" Erban took a sip of coffee. "We could play cards at night," he added halfheartedly.

She gazed at the rain dripping off the eaves, unable to get the Murphy farm out of her mind.

"We'll get by, Lizzy," Erban said. "I still got all the encyclopedias in my room."

She looked at him. "What?"

"My daddy's books. Remember we saved them?"

"Erban, those damn books of yours are more boring than watching snow. I don't care about something that happened hundreds of years ago in a place I never heard of."

Erban looked hurt. "I like them."

"I know you do. Anyway, I can't read that well in the first place."

"I could teach you."

"I don't care to improve my reading any." She raised her cup, watching him over the brim. "Have you thought anymore about the offer?"

"Offer?"

"The Copperhead."

"Harlan said he turned them down. He doesn't want to move."

"What about you?" She patted his hand. "Have you ever thought about moving to a nicer place?"

"I never thought about moving at all."

She bit her lip. "Well, think about it."

He shrugged.

"Think harder, Erban. We could live in a house that's not falling down. We could have indoor bathrooms."

"It sounds nice."

"Nice? Picture living in a place where the roof didn't leak. The basement didn't flood. We could have a living room with a floor again, for God's sake."

The door in the hall banged open. Harlan wandered into the room, expelling air. He walked to the sink and spat. "Rained the bastards out, I bet."

Elizabeth stared at him.

"The coal people," Harlan said. "The bastards can't work in weather like this. That damn shovel ain't running today." He reached a mug from the cupboard and poured coffee. "Don't eat all of them," he said as Elizabeth brought a donut to her mouth.

"There's more."

"More bought with my money. And this coffee is too damn strong. How many times do I have to tell you about it?"

"A billion and one," she said, popping the remaining half of the donut into her mouth.

The rain continued throughout the day—one minute a mist, moments later pounding down as if to wash the house away. Water dripped through holes in the old roof. Erban took several pots and pans upstairs to his parents' musty rooms. He arranged the containers around the floor to catch the steady flow.

By late afternoon the storm had moved south. Scattered bars of sunshine extended through breaks in the clouds. To Erban the sight resembled a scene from *The Ten Commandments:* columns of light spreading like a fan, the angels about to descend from heaven.

In the kitchen Erban stood at the window. Harlan paced across the floor, stopping now and then to point at his wife.

"They are out digging again. I know it."

"There's nothing we can do about it," Elizabeth said.

Harlan scowled.

Elizabeth stood up. She moved heavily to the icebox and took out a plate of sliced ham. "Why don't we just move?"

"What?" Harlan stood motionless in the middle of the floor.

"Why don't we move? We could get a place on Crooked Run."

A vein on Harlan's temple throbbed. "You are the stupidest woman I've ever seen."

"I'm the only woman you've ever seen." Elizabeth spread the ham in the hot pan. "Besides your mother."

Harlan stepped closer to Elizabeth. "Don't you know the money we'd get wouldn't buy squat? That ain't as much money as it sounds. We'd owe money and we wouldn't have any left to eat with."

"You could work maybe."

"I don't goddamn want to. I never goddamn have."

"Maybe we could at least look for a place?" Erban knew he should keep his mouth shut. His stomach tightened. "We might find something cheap."

Harlan swiped at one of the kitchen chairs. "See what you've done? Now my brother's an idiot, too. Listen, you two want to find a place they're giving away for free, go at it. This is where I was born and this is where I intend to die."

"Well, hurry up with it then so the rest of us can live." Elizabeth waved the large serving fork. "There are other people in this house, you know."

"Other people I've been feeding."

Elizabeth laughed. "You know what I think about that one."

Erban watched his brother's face darken. It seemed as if something low and mean and full of hurt had swept into the room. He moved for the door and turned the knob. "I'm going out," he said, though he knew no one was listening.

The sun held low in the sky. Gold light slanted through the clouds, illuminating the distant hill. Erban sighed. When it came to Harlan and Elizabeth, he didn't know who to believe. His brother always acted so sure of things. He spoke each word as if it were absolute truth. But Elizabeth's idea made sense, too. It hadn't occurred to him they could actually move. He'd always liked those farms out on Crooked Run. If they moved over there, he'd be closer to his insulator hunting.

Inside the house, Harlan and Elizabeth were shouting and banging things around. Erban wondered if they would hurt each other some day. Their fights made him sick, as if he'd been hit hard in the stomach. Sometimes he couldn't breathe until he was far from the house.

Erban walked down the muddy lane. Scores of brown streams crisscrossed the ground. The water flowed steadily as it sought the creek behind the Beitzal place, and further on the Sugarcreek River.

Nearing the abandoned Slater farm, Erban slowed. The house and barn sat off the road in a low flat meadow. Beyond the bare fields the land hunched steeply into a wooded hill. Willy Slater had built the house and outbuildings years ago, long before Erban had been born. The Slater farm had been the first on the lane.

In high school Erban had always searched for Mary Slater whenever he passed the farm, perhaps a glimpse of her as she came back from closing the chicken house for the night. Sometimes she would sit on the porch after supper, working on pieces to a patchwork quilt. She always waved if she saw him on the road.

One afternoon, Mrs. Hanson had asked them to decorate the classroom for Easter. They were both seniors that year. She said they were her best students in Art, then left them alone with a tablet of construction paper and a box of supplies.

They sat in the rear of the empty classroom. Mary's hair, the color of straw, was gathered and tied on top of her head. Erban thought she looked already grown-up, as if she knew something about life that he hadn't yet learned.

"Why Erban Kern," she said, tugging playfully on his arm, "you are the most quiet boy I've ever seen. My brothers wake up shouting and don't stop until they're asleep at night."

Erban swallowed hard. "I'm afraid of you." The words had flown from his mouth. He put down the scissors, embarrassed.

"Erban," she said, smiling, "why on earth would you be afraid of me?"

"Because you're different." He thought that didn't sound right. "You're nice."

"What do you mean?"

"You don't tease me like the others." He glanced at the scarred table. "I like talking to you."

Mary waited until he looked up. "I like talking to you, too." She glued a cotton ball onto the cutout of a rabbit. "What else do you like?"

"I like to watch the sky."

"Erban Kern, you are one unusual bean. My brothers have never noticed the sky, unless it threatened rain and there was hay in the field."

"I like the high clouds best. The ones that look as if they are near the sun. They look like a spider's web."

"Have you ever talked to Mrs. Hanson? She knows a lot about how clouds are formed, their different names."

"I don't like school," he said. "People are too mean."

In the silent room, she touched his hand.

Erban reached the end of the muddy lane with the image of Mary still in his head. It was a memory he treasured, a moment recalled as easily as someone might pull out an old photograph. Before him Crooked Run twisted into the distance, the pavement clean and black from the rain. He turned right and set off down the road.

The windows of the Martin house glared in the setting sun. Erban poked his head in the open doorway. "Anybody home?" he called.

Ida Martin tottered into the room. She moved slowly, as if unsure of her legs, leaning against different pieces of furniture as she struggled toward him. Erban studied the dirty Ace bandages around her ankles. Over the years since the Martins had moved into the Specht house, Erban had seen her only a few times from the road. He took an involuntary step back.

"Are you the new Stanley Brush Man?" she asked, her words shaped by a thick German accent.

"Dayton Specht sent me down. He said to talk with your husband about some insulators."

"Hans is out back with Fritz and our granddaughter." She rested against the bookcase. "My legs aren't none too good. I busted a vein in my foot last week. I wouldn't have known it, except for the wetness in my shoe, my sock just sliding around."

Erban took off his hat. He resisted an urge to bolt through the door. "Is it true there are insulators here?"

"That's right." The bookcase groaned as Ida shifted her weight. "When we moved in they were everywhere."

"Can I see them?"

Ida pointed over her shoulder. "Go through the kitchen there to the back door. Hans will show you where they are." She frowned. "What do you want with them anyway?"

"I collect them."

"Seems like a funny thing to collect. My son, Walt, used to have a train set. He bought all the cars and engines. Built little bridges and towns and water towers, exactly like the real things. Would you care to see it? We still have it in the attic."

"I got to get back before dark."

"Who are you anyway? Are you a Vogel?"

"I'm a Kern. I live out Willy Slater's Lane."

Ida let loose of the bookcase and reached out for him. "Help me over to the chair."

The woman hooked her arm over his shoulders. He grunted as her weight pressed down, his thighs quivering. Her sour breath stung his eyes. At the chair they turned in small steps so Ida could sit. The floor shook as she plopped down.

"That's better," she said. She looked up as if she'd just remembered something. "I didn't think anyone lived on Willy Slater's Lane anymore. Hans told me they're stripping out there. I see the coal trucks all the time."

"My brother and me are the only ones left. The coal people want to buy us out." Erban put on his hat and started for the kitchen. "I'll go now."

"Don't let that big shovel gobble you up," she said, propping her thick legs on a hassock. She looked out the window. "They'll carry you off some day in one of those semi trucks."

Erban nodded on his way out the door.

Hans Martin sat under the grape arbor in the yard. Beside him stood a younger man holding a baby. Erban removed his hat again.

"Erban Kern, is it?" Hans pointed at him. "I always see you out walking. Dayton said you might come for those old insulators. This is Fritz and his little girl. Gretta's three weeks old."

Erban took a wary step forward. The baby peeked at him from a blanket covered with dancing bears.

"She can smile already," Fritz Martin said.

Erban stared at the infant. He couldn't remember ever seeing a child that age. "She's so small."

"Hold out your finger," Hans said. "She'll grab it like the dickens."

Erban extended a crooked finger, cautiously, as if the baby would bite. He jumped when she gripped him with her tiny hand. "She's strong."

"She's a Martin," Hans said, standing. "She's got Swiss blood in her."

Fritz pulled the blanket around the baby's chin. "I'm supposed to watch the evening air. Becky says she can catch cold easily, she's so young."

Erban tried to pull away, but the baby wouldn't let go of his hand. Wisps of fear encircled his heart. He tugged again and the little fingers continued to hold. "She's really got me."

"She likes you, Erban," Hans said. "She's the friendliest little one I've ever seen."

Erban jerked his finger free and pushed both hands deep into his pockets.

"Do you have any children?" Fritz asked.

Erban stared at the man's face. "I ain't even got a wife."

"Let's look at those insulators," Hans said. "I've got them in here." He opened the door to the building behind them.

Broken furniture and junk filled the room. In one corner an iron stove sat covered in dust. Several worn-out bicycles, some missing wheels, others without seats, lay strewn across the floor. Along the far wall, cans of paint were stacked beside a rolltop desk. Hans led the way through the maze.

"They're back here near the window," he said, stepping over a doll without a head, its plastic arms covered in dirt. "Here they are."

Erban peered over the older man's shoulder. Hundreds of insulators covered a stained mattress on the floor. This was even greater than he had dared hope. The base of his scalp tingled. His own collection didn't compare to the treasure before him.

"Don't know what you see in these things." Hans shrugged. "They're yours if you want. I just use them for shooting practice sometimes." He shuffled across the cluttered room and went outside.

Erban knelt on the cement floor, his hands shaking. For a moment he thought he might faint. One of the insulators caught his eye. He studied its smooth lines in the fading light. Small, about the size of his fist, the insulator was round on top, flaring to a wider bottom piece. He carefully picked it up. None of the brown paint had been chipped away. He would take this one for sure. He sat with his back against the wall and held the insulator like a prize, testing its weight, admiring the solid compact feel.

The young Martin child broke into his thoughts—how the baby had studied him, eyes reflecting the red dusk. The way she'd gripped his finger. Erban trembled in the growing dark. An odd sensation misted over him like fog.

He looked up.

Someone stood in the feathery shadows across the room. Erban stared, rubbed both eyes. It was himself, as a much younger man. Beside the young Erban stood a boy of three or four, holding a model car. A girl of about the same age stepped from the darkness, then another. Both wore brightly colored ribbons in their yellow hair. The girls joined hands and began to dance. They smiled at the young Erban, gently called his name.

Erban sat beside the mattress. He wanted to look away, but couldn't. The girls spun in a whirl of summer dresses, moving faster and faster until they began to lose their balance. The young Erban reached out too late. The girls staggered and fell, their bodies shattering on the hard concrete. Arms and legs broke cleanly from their sockets. Streams of black erupted from the crushed heads, pooling on the floor. A single hand, motionless like a forgotten glove, lay near the rolltop desk.

The boy with the model car whimpered.

"No," Erban whispered. He shut his eyes tightly, rested his head against his knees. In vain he willed the children away. He wanted no part of this. Then, as fast as they had swept into the room, the people vanished. He saw nothing but the faint outlines of the furniture. The bent and twisted bicycle frames. The insulator was heavy in his hand.

Erban groped around for the mattress. He put the insulator on the pile and stood up. Extending his hands like a blind man, he stumbled toward the door. He bumped into something heavy and moved to the side, tripped over something else at his feet. As he neared the open door, someone turned on the flood light outside. Erban sprinted into the yard.

"There you are," Hans said. "I forgot to tell you where the light was."

Erban started for the road. "I got to go before it gets too dark."

"What about those insulators?"

"I don't need any right now," he said without stopping. "I got enough around."

He rushed along the side of the house. The windows cast yellow squares on the grass. Spooked by the sounds of the coming night, he started for home.

Around the Kern farm that summer nothing moved. Not a hint of wind came out of the hills. Harlan and Erban and Elizabeth sat on the porch, fanning themselves with old copies of *The Watchtower* magazine. They slapped at horseflies buzzing tirelessly through the air.

At the mouth of the lane the dragline worked on, lifting out the dark coal. The Kerns listened to the digging machine through the heavy air: the constant grind and clunk as the boom pivoted, the swell of the engine when the bucket raked the ground. The loaded trucks growled as they started for the processing mine on Route 21.

One evening toward dusk, Harlan stood above what had been Hank Slater's pasture land. He'd hiked over to the top of the hill before supper, curious to see how far the stripping operation had advanced.

In the clearing below, the dragline swung its boom in a wide arc. Ink-dark smoke stained the sky. Harlan watched as the enormous bucket clawed another swath. The machine looked like some monster from the bedtime stories his mother had told, the kind of beast that lumbered through the countryside, stomping on houses and eating everything in sight. The dragline was even bigger than he had thought, as tall and wide as a three-story house. The bucket alone could easily swallow several pickup trucks.

"Goddamn," Harlan said, impressed. "Goddamn it to hell and back." He crouched behind a stump, watching the men hustle about in the waning light. The workers resembled busy insects, swarming the bulldozers and graders and trucks, hanging from the long boom. Behind the dragline the earth rose in colorless mounds, each towering thirty feet or more.

As Harlan watched, the frenzied activity diminished. The operation was halting for the night. After a few minutes, the dragline shut down. The last of the semi trucks rumbled down the access road, the crew wandering to their pickups, leaving for home. From a trailer at the side of the clearing, a man emerged and stood smoking a cigarette. He strolled to the last remaining truck. He circled the area once before driving away.

Harlan waited a moment before picking his way down the hillside. He worked hard to avoid the stumps and fallen branches. At the bottom of the hill he leaned against a cotton-wood, his heart clanging beneath his shirt.

Harlan stumbled through the undergrowth at the edge of the clearing. He glanced around, then stepped out into the open, hurrying between the bulldozers and other heavy equipment. He stopped beside the towering bulk of the dragline. The bucket had been swung outward before the engine was killed, coming to rest deep in the ground. Harlan looked around once more. He climbed the metal ladder to the cockpit, surprised to find the door open. He ducked low and stepped inside.

The small enclosure had a cozy feel. Harlan eased onto the operator's seat, the chair more comfortable than expected. He swiveled left, then right, pulling on the various levers, pushing buttons and flicking switches. Nothing happened. He tried to imagine what it was like to spend entire days at the controls—logging the countless hours, driving off each evening covered in coal dust.

Soon the dragline would approach the farmhouses built along the lane: the Slaters, the Beitzals, the Hermanns. Harlan slumped in the chair. Elizabeth was dead wrong about starting over. No one, he was sure, had ever changed anything by moving to a different place. Living remained the same wherever you did it.

Harlan examined the intricate control board. He could yank out some wires, perhaps. Smash switches and dials with his boots. He stood and opened the door instead, stepping onto the top rung of the ladder. Nothing would do any good. The Copperhead would simply fix the dragline and continue working. *At least they won't get my place,* he thought. *At least not that.* With the rim of the moon rising above the black trees, Harlan started for home.

At the farm, Erban sat on the porch with Volume One of the Encyclopaedia Britannica. *Aardvark to Aztec* was stenciled in gold across the imitation leather cover. Fireflies sparked over the yard in bright yellow-green. This evening Erban read about Chester Arthur, the twenty-first president of the United States. He'd never heard of President Arthur, but that was why he read. Each time he went through his books he learned something new. Reading made him feel more substantial, as if the extra knowledge added weight upon his bones.

The porch light snapped on. Elizabeth opened the screen door and stepped outside. "How can you read in the dark?"

"I like to read in the last light. For a few moments the words glow on the page."

Elizabeth sat in the rocker beside him. "Half the time I don't understand what you mean, but I still like hearing you speak."

Erban flipped to a different place in the book. The picture showed a handsome man with dark eyes. ALEXANDER THE GREAT, the caption said, 356–323 B.C., KING OF MACEDONIA. "Harlan should be home soon."

"Supper's ready now if you want."

"I don't think Harlan would like that."

Elizabeth laughed. "Harlan doesn't like much of anything— you and me included. If he had a way to get food and have his underwear washed he'd be alone right now."

"He cares about us."

"Cares my ass, Erban." She touched his arm. "He tolerates us because he has to. To him we just eat up groceries. Deplete the supplies of toilet paper and soap. He'd much rather keep that last bit of money buried in the ground. It saves his ass from having to work."

Erban closed the book on his lap. He rubbed his hands across the cover, admiring the raised surface of the letters. He pressed the book against him, enjoying its heft and solidness. Sometimes he simply buried his nose into the pages, breathing in the smell of the yellowed paper. Here were real answers, actual facts. He felt powerless against what Elizabeth was telling him. Ideas you couldn't decide were true or not. If only he had a book to help him with those things, too.

Elizabeth sighed. "Have you thought any more about that offer? The Copperhead said we could still sell if we wanted to."

"You spoke with them?"

"Yesterday in town." She lowered her voice. "They have an office on Maple Street. I stopped on my way back from the store."

Erban was stunned. Harlan had warned her against stopping anywhere besides Kroger's. Or Mobil Oil when the truck needed gas. "What did they say?"

"They said you own half this place. It should be partly your decision." Elizabeth turned her bulk in the chair. "Don't you want to get out of this hole? We've got our couch in the kitchen, for christsakes."

"It's not so bad."

"It's not that great, either. The Murphy farm is still for sale. They have a well-kept house, more land. We could actually farm for a change. Keep some cattle and chickens."

Erban watched a scattering of bats emerge from the barn. They lurched crazily above the yard, disappearing in an instant into the expanding dark. "Harlan doesn't like farming."

"What about you?"

Erban remembered trying to help his father. Nothing had been accomplished without effort and pain. His dad could do the farm work with absolute ease, as if it were second nature. "I was never much good at it. My father never made me do much. He thought I was too skinny."

"It's exasperating to talk with you sometimes." Elizabeth pounded down the front steps. She marched halfway into the yard and turned. "We could actually work with our hands. Don't you see we could accomplish something?"

Erban studied his hands on the cover of the book, his skin pale under the light. Once more he felt the old confusion return. What Elizabeth said made sense. It might be good to try farming again.

"Would we have to get jobs?" he asked. "Like Harlan says?"

"Working won't kill us. We could each do a little odd job to bring in extra cash. At least till the farm started making money. I could even waitress at that new Amish restaurant. I already know how."

Elizabeth walked to the porch rail. She reached out and rested her hand on his knee. "It'd be a new life for us."

His stomach hurt. The new ideas whirled through his head, tumbling together until he was dizzy.

"It sounds all right," he said.

"What sounds all right?" Harlan stood at the edge of the yard. "Get your goddamn hand off my brother's knee."

Elizabeth's mouth set in a hard line. She walked up the steps and into the house without saying a word.

"What the hell was that? She after your bony ass?"

Erban looked back at the house. From inside the kitchen the oven door screeched on its hinges. "She was wondering what we were going to do."

"Do about what?" Harlan leaned against the porch rail, taking the place Elizabeth had been. "What did she say?"

"She said we could start over again."

"Why would we want to do that?"

Erban stared down the lane. The trees had melted into an indistinguishable wall of blackness. He didn't like the tone in his brother's voice. Soon would come the shouts, the threats. "She thought maybe we could live a little better."

"Lookit. We don't have to work. We live away from people and their snoopy-assed noses. This is what most Americans would die to have."

"We could own more land like we used to. Grow crops."

"Jesus H. Christ." Harlan kicked at one of the beams supporting the porch. "Lizzy's got your head screwed ass-backwards again. We're too old to work, even if we wanted to. We've got to stay here."

Erban shifted uneasily in his chair. "She was just thinking out loud."

"That kind of thinking will send us down a greased pole to hell. You leave the thinking to me. I'll see we do the right thing."

Harlan climbed the three porch steps. He stood beside Erban's chair, looking down. "We understand each other. Don't we?"

Erban nodded. He remembered the hundreds of times his brother had towered over him, just as he was now.

"I can't hear you."

Bright sparks of anger flared in Erban's chest. He closed his eyes, pulling air into his lungs until the heat faded away.

"I understand," he said. He listened to Harlan clomp into the house. Opening his eyes he saw his hands gripping the book, knuckles white as bone.

Harlan found Elizabeth sitting at the kitchen table. His pulse surged through his ears. "You leave my brother alone, goddamn it. You'll get him all confused."

"You're the one who's confused."

He grabbed a plate and flung it across the room. It exploded against the far wall, sugaring the couch with glass.

"That was your favorite plate, Harlan. You can eat off the table tonight."

"Son of a royal bitch." He gripped Elizabeth under the arm, tried to wrench her from the seat. She wouldn't budge.

"Don't hurt yourself," she said.

His hands moved on their own. He snagged a thick handful of hair, yanking back her head. A frantic hand clawed for his face. Her elbow swung around. He increased the tension until she stopped struggling.

"This is the last I want to hear about moving. This is the last I want to hear about anything."

Her breath stalled.

"Is that a yes?"

Elizabeth didn't answer. She stared at him with her mouth closed. The look in her eyes was something he hadn't seen before—an expression of absolute rage, as if she could kill him where he stood. She unnerved him. He let go of her hair and stepped back.

"Clean up the broken glass," he said, walking heavy-footed to the front door. He stopped with his hand on the knob. "You and Erban eat. I'm not hungry."

At the end of summer, Harlan sat on the couch in the kitchen. He watched Elizabeth snap beans for supper, admiring her broad backside as it moved under her dress. "We've got to celebrate, Lizzy. Bring me one of the Rolling Rocks from the fridge."

Elizabeth gave him a hard stare. She opened the refrigerator and grabbed a beer, then tossed the green bottle across the room. Harlan caught the beer in mid-air.

"Don't be so pissed," he said. "This really isn't such a bad place."

That afternoon, a representative from the Copperhead Coal Company had made a final offer for the farm. Harlan had turned him down.

"You realize, Mr. Kern," the man had said, standing beside the tractor frame, "that this whole area will soon be under excavation. The dragline itself will be practically in your front yard. The living conditions would be totally unacceptable."

"The way I figure, you can't come within a couple hundred yards of my house. The property line runs from that beech tree over there to the mailbox." Harlan noted the sweat beading across the man's forehead. "You'll be far enough away."

He laughed out loud as the car drove away.

On the couch, Harlan took a cold sip of beer. Elizabeth was flipping hamburgers in the iron skillet, the meat sizzling with a satisfying sound. "I guess you won't be getting the Murphy place."

Elizabeth calmly lifted the skillet from the stove. She walked to the couch, holding the handle with both hands. Grease sputtered over the side as she stood above him. He could hear the hot meat still cooking in its juices.

"Don't gloat so much, Harlan. Just leave it alone."

Harlan leaned back as far as he could. "All right, Lizzy." A sputter of grease arced onto his knee. "You mind getting that goddamn thing away from me?"

Elizabeth paused before turning around. At the table, she placed a burger on each of the plates. "This is better than I had at home, but not as good as it gets."

"That's a matter of perspective," Harlan said, raising the bottle in the gesture of a toast. "It depends entirely on how you look at things."

On a Friday afternoon in mid-November, Elizabeth Kern drove the old Ford pickup into town. She sat solidly in the mashed-down seat, the steering wheel against her bust. Cold air whistled through rust holes in the frame. The truck swerved as hair blew across her face.

Elizabeth passed the huge billboard before town: *Welcome to Sugarcreek, the Little Switzerland of Ohio.* Painted above the caption, an Alpine shepherd bowed at the waist with a feathered cap in his hand. She smiled as she passed the sign. The shepherd made her feel as if she were entering a foreign city. She imagined a place where dashing young men roamed the streets, tipping their caps to the ladies.

At the intersection of Adler and Main, Elizabeth turned left through the center of town. She passed the chalet-style buildings lining the street. This was her favorite part of the drive. She enjoyed the displays in the shop windows. Elizabeth inspected both sides of the street, careful not to miss anything.

In the window of Andreas Furniture, a sleigh sat loaded with brightly wrapped gifts. A life-sized mechanical Santa Claus waved at her, turning stiffly from side to side. Elizabeth stopped in the middle of the street. Behind her someone honked their horn.

"In your ear," she mumbled, easing out the clutch. The truck jumped forward with a jerk.

At Kroger's she parked near a row of Amish buggies. She stood a moment beside the truck. The breath from the horses formed great clouds in the air. She shivered and gathered her shawl around her throat.

Elizabeth kept her eyes averted inside the store. She never looked at anyone directly—that would mean returning some sign of recognition. In her three years of isolation at the Kern house, she'd lost the ability to function in public. Even a simple greeting came with difficulty. It was best to avoid as much contact with people as possible.

Elizabeth looked at the list Harlan had scrawled on the edge of a grocery sack: baked beans, canned corn, bread, butter, eggs. She found the idea of a list funny. Harlan always wanted the same things, as constant as the seasons. Erban ate whatever she put in front of him.

Someone tapped her shoulder near the canned vegetables. A woman with white hair watched her through thick glasses. Her skin looked rough and windburned—a farmer's wife.

"Are you Mrs. Kern?" she asked, her eyebrows lifting with the question.

Elizabeth nodded.

"I'm Cora Specht, Dayton's wife. My husband bought land from your husband years ago. We live near the turnoff for Willy Slater's Lane."

"I know where you live."

Cora Specht hesitated. "We were wondering how everyone was doing."

Elizabeth checked her list. For a moment her vision blurred.

She wished the woman would go away. She wanted to finish shopping and start for the house.

"Dayton said Harlan turned down the coal people. He said you folks are going to stay."

"My husband's a fucking idiot," Elizabeth said.

Cora Specht winced. "Well, I just wanted to say hello. Dayton and I were hoping everything was good." She gave a weak smile. "We never see you people much—only Erban when he's out walking. You and Harlan are welcome to come anytime."

"We don't get out much," Elizabeth said, dropping three cans of corn into her cart. She wheeled away without looking back.

On the way home, Elizabeth went over the conversation in her head. The woman hadn't meant any harm. Mrs. Specht was simply being nice. *I act like my husband,* she thought. She had actually enjoyed shocking the woman. *I'll be as mean as the old bastard before it's all said and done.*

Turning onto Crooked Run, she began to shudder. Violent chills ran through her. Her arms trembled without warning, the truck veering across the center line and then back again. Gusts of cold wind swirled the cab. She drifted right, almost taking out a mailbox. Goose bumps prickled her arms and legs. *Damn hunk of junk.* Her teeth chattered. *Worthless heap of useless tin.*

By the time she reached Willy Slater's Lane, her eyes could barely focus. She wondered if she would make it home. At last she pulled into the front yard. Her head pounded with the beat of her heart. She rolled onto the seat and closed her eyes.

Erban walked along the south end of Crooked Run, searching the grass. It was time for him to turn back. Glancing up he found himself well beyond the Martin place, its silos dark against the falling sun. He turned around and headed for the house. When Erban got home, Harlan was sitting alone in the kitchen.

"Lizzy's taken to her bed." He didn't look up from the newspaper. "Says she's too sick for her chores. You'll have to cook for yourself."

Erban hung up his coat. He felt a strange fluttering sensation in his stomach, like hundreds of tiny moths had been turned loose inside him.

"What's the matter with her?"

Harlan scowled into his paper. "I ain't no doctor, Erban. I'll tell you what I told her. Chills and fever are mostly in the mind."

At the wood stove, Erban smeared lard into the iron skillet. He looked down the hall to the closed bedroom door, wondering if Elizabeth were okay. He stole a glance at his brother. Harlan held the newspaper at arm's length, angled to the light.

"Do you think she's hungry?" Erban asked.

"Don't worry about her none."

"I could make an extra egg."

Harlan peeked over the top of his paper. "Is your hearing bad? If she wants to lay in bed like an old sow, then let her. There's no use encouraging her to be lazy."

Erban peppered the eggs in the skillet. He didn't know what to say.

"Is there now?" Harlan asked.

"I guess not," Erban said.

The next morning, Erban filled the bucket from the pump and carried it inside. Harlan sat by himself in the kitchen. He didn't move from his chair.

"Lizzy still in bed?" Erban asked.

"She's just sulking cause we didn't sell the farm. She's no sicker than me or you."

"But she did look pale yesterday," Erban said, testing his brother.

Harlan jumped to his feet. "You saying I don't know my own wife?"

Erban raised both arms to cover his face. He cautiously brought them down. As he turned to the stove, concern for Elizabeth continued to pester him.

"But what if she is bad?"

Harlan strode across the floor. "She's *my* wife." His eyes narrowed. "Just leave my business to me."

Erban flinched. His brother was acting even angrier than usual. He seemed about to explode.

Harlan walked to his chair, then stopped and whirled around. "You just stay away from Lizzy now," he shouted. "I'll bring her in line."

Erban turned back to the stove. Something inside him would not let the discussion end. "You can kill her, too," he said, under his breath.

"What was that?"

"I said she might die."

Harlan broke into a fit a laughter. "That woman is as strong as a bull. She isn't about to keel over from a runny nose."

"How can you be sure?"

"Leave it alone, Erban." The darkness returned to Harlan's face. "This doesn't concern you." He jerked open the front door and flung it shut behind him.

Harlan spent the day outside. Erban heard him banging things around, cursing the air. His brother sounded as if he were in a fight. Erban stayed on the couch, reading about the American Revolution. His mind continually wandered from Benjamin Franklin and the Treaty of Paris.

Daylight waned outside the dusty windows. Shadows crawled the floor. Erban turned on the overhead light and stood blinking at the brightness. With a sneer on his face, Harlan finished supper. Erban didn't ask about making something for Elizabeth. His brother was not in the mood to be crossed.

After washing the dishes, Erban eased into the rocker on the porch. Faint stars outlined the clouds. His parents had sat on the porch every night. Erban could still see his father studying the sky as the constellations wheeled overhead. Mother always joined him after the kitchen work. The two talked for hours, their voices low, while Erban listened from his room. The sound of their words made him feel safe. He had assumed his parents would be there forever.

The night rolled away from his feet, silent and deep. He felt alone, acutely isolated, the only person alive in the stretch of blackness. Not a light shone anywhere. He could have been on a ship at sea with land nothing but a distant hope. Erban shook his head. He gazed at the dark hulks of the farm equipment in the yard. He crossed his arms against the cold.

The porch light snapped on. Harlan stepped outside, pulling the door shut with a bang. He stood next to Erban and stared into the night.

"Colder than a witch's tit," he said finally. "It'll snow before Thanksgiving."

"Maybe so."

Harlan chuckled. "Remember the time we went sled riding with the old man? That steep hill behind the Hermann place?" Puffs of breath faded and were gone.

Erban recalled the day instantly. They had hiked over after a three-day storm, climbing to the hilltop in an icy wind. Below them the countryside spread outward in a sheet of white. Silver clouds hung scalloped across the sky like the layered scales of a fish. He held onto his brother with all his strength as they sped down the hill.

"I was scared. I didn't like it."

Harlan leaned against the porch rail. "To tell you the truth, I was scared shitless." He spat into the yard. "Never knew that did you?"

Erban shrugged his shoulders. He wondered what his brother was getting at. Harlan rarely spoke with him in this way.

"You know the only reason I didn't wreck us?"

44

"No."

"Because I knew you were depending on me." Harlan patted him once on the back. "I knew I had to get us to the bottom of that hill."

"You didn't like it?"

"I thought we were going to die. My hands were slipping and we kept picking up speed. I knew if we wrecked we'd break our necks. When I felt you shaking behind me, I somehow grabbed on tighter. I felt like I could hold on forever."

"I didn't know."

"There's a lot you don't know, Erban." Harlan turned and went inside. The porch light clicked off.

In the darkness Erban tilted his head to the side, deep in thought. He wasn't sure what had just happened between them. At times Harlan seemed as mysterious as the distant stars. Erban took a cold breath and let it out. He wondered if he would ever come close to understanding his brother.

Over the next week Erban and Harlan moved around their house warily, mindful of each other. The sound of coughing filtered constantly through the closed bedroom door. Sometimes Elizabeth called out, but for what Erban could not hear.

Once a day Harlan took food into his wife: a hunk of cheese, a can of beans, some bread. He went into the room and shut the door, returning minutes later with a scowl. By the end of the week, he had stopped taking her something to eat.

"She'll come out when she's hungry enough," he said. "She could stand to lose a few pounds, anyway. That woman weighs a ton."

Erban looked up from his book. "I don't think this is right."

"What?" Harlan stood in the middle of the floor, legs splayed as if ready for battle.

"Nothing," Erban said.

On Friday morning, Harlan got ready to take the truck into

town. "Hope I remember how to drive," he said, pulling on his coat. "Anything special we need?"

Erban shook his head.

"Now you leave her be," Harlan said, pausing with his hand on the door. "You stay out of my room."

Erban waited until the pickup faded from sight. He knocked on the bedroom door. When Elizabeth didn't answer, he turned the knob and went inside. She lay in a tangle of damp sheets and blankets. Her sweat-soaked gown clung to her skin, hugging the shape of her breasts. Heat seemed to rise from her body into the cold room.

"Lizzy?" he asked, tentatively.

Elizabeth turned in the direction of his voice. She tried to speak. She struggled through a long spell of coughing instead.

Erban drew closer. "What's that?"

"Help me."

"What can I do?"

She didn't seem to hear him. Her eyes slowly closed.

Erban looked around the room. Shirts and pants and dresses spilled from open drawers onto the floor. Next to the closet sat a full bedpan. His stomach wavered at the smell. The mattress springs squeaked as Elizabeth coughed again.

Erban walked straight out of the room. He grabbed his coat and took off down the lane as quickly as he could. He didn't stop until he was at Dayton Specht's front door.

"I've come to use the phone," he said.

5 Doc Krantz stood at the window of his office in downtown Sugarcreek. He squinted into the bright afternoon. Windblown tourists roamed the sidewalks, bundled in their coats. *If it gets any colder,* he thought, *they'll freeze their asses right off.* He wiped his spectacles on his handkerchief. Across the street, the revolving sign at the bank read ten degrees.

The doctor watched a Lincoln Continental park at the curb. A family of six scrambled out. They leaned into the wind, shielding their faces with matching scarves. Each member wore a different size of the same coat. "Tourists," he grumbled.

Doc Krantz remembered sadly the way the town had looked forty years ago, when he'd first opened his practice. At the time only three hundred people had lived in Sugarcreek, the majority of the residents from Switzerland. The townsfolk were hard-working men and women, as industrious and frugal as any people Krantz had seen. Each house looked as solid as the families living inside them.

Back then, Sugarcreek consisted of a Swiss cheese dairy, an auction barn, a handful of shops, and a train depot. The general store stocked everything a man could want, including oil lanterns and bolts of black cloth for the hundreds of local Amish farms. From the start Doc Krantz had admired the Amish for their plain houses and barns, each building neat and trim. The Amish worked as hard as the immigrants in town.

But during the last ten years, Sugarcreek had changed. He'd known at once it was a mistake: the merchants promoting the Swiss heritage of the town the way products are sold on TV. The whole transformation had begun with a small festival held one Friday in September. On a blustery afternoon, the merchants closed off Main Street and erected booths for food and crafts. For a few hours the local townspeople walked around in traditional Swiss clothing, listening to Alpine music piped through loudspeakers. Neighbors chatted about the homeland and drank imported beer. The second year, Ivan Mueller from the cheese house donated money to build a stage. Local bands played while people danced the polka in the streets. The festival extended over the weekend, ending with a yodeling contest in which Frederick Shutz won a thirty-pound wheel of cheese.

In the years that followed, word of the quaint little festival spread through the neighboring counties. Attendance swelled from a few dozen local residents to thousands of people from around the state. Klaus Shumacher remodeled the front of the general store, building the facade of a Swiss chalet across its front, complete with scalloped trim and flower boxes in the windows. He stocked not only his regular merchandise, but fancy cuckoo clocks imported from his cousin in Geneva, carved wooden bears from his uncle in Bern.

The other store owners followed suit. By the end of the third year, Main Street looked like something from the Swiss Alps. The merchants crammed their windows full of imports, everything from Swiss Army knives and watches to fondue cookbooks and tapes of championship yodeling. The entire business made Doc Krantz uneasy. At first he'd refused to have the front of his store redone in such a ridiculous way—as if he knew any more about Switzerland than the tourists gawking in the streets. Finally, the other store owners pooled their money for the remodeling. Unable to look at their disappointed faces, he gave his consent. He sat inside his office during the construction, shaking his head.

Doc Krantz wasn't sure why the whole thing bothered him so much. No one was hurt by the town's different look, not even the flight of tourists migrating there spring through late fall. The ruse was harmless enough. It even made the poor city folks happy. Maybe what troubled him was that the place he had admired was gone. On his first day in town, Sugarcreek had captured his heart with its gritty determination. Now Doc Krantz had the notion the community was growing soft. Most of the residents seemed happy to live off the money of other people, the way a parasite lives off other living things.

Sometimes, as he drove home in the evening, the whole street looked like Disney World to him. A trick to the eye. Red and white Swiss flags waving next to Old Glory. Alpine murals on the side of the town hall. Sugarcreek relied on illusion as much as any ride at that famous amusement park.

Several years ago, Doc Krantz had gone down to Florida with a group from church. *An adventure in magic,* the brochure had said. He stood around in the hot sun for an hour to go on a five-minute ride, wondering what all the fuss was about. Finally, Emerson Young pointed to an empty bench under a shade tree. The two let the group continue without them, content to miss the best Fantasyland had to offer.

"I just don't get it, Emerson," he said, leaning back against the bench. "The whole place's built on making you think you are some place you're not."

Emerson took off his shoes. He looked ready to keel over from heat prostration. "That's the idea," he said.

Watching the town gradually change, Doc Krantz decided

Sugarcreek had indeed become some sort of Fantasyland—and he was part of it, lost somewhere between the cheese house tour and the live blacksmithing demonstration every day at noon.

An Amish buggy wheeled down the street, stopping at the light. The horse waited patiently while a snake of cars passed before it. Even the Amish were a disappointment to Doc Krantz anymore. With their new barn-size restaurant on Route 39, they catered to the tour buses that roared through the area. He'd heard from his patients an Amish quilt shop would open soon beside the Goshen Dairy. *Next they'll be giving buggy rides for five dollars a shot.* He turned from the window. *I'm just a cranky old man today.*

Someone knocked on the office door, faintly at first, then more forcefully. The doctor pushed his spectacles higher onto his nose. He sat down behind his desk.

"Come," he said.

A woman with bleached hair poked her head into the room. She glanced around, then stepped inside.

"Are you the doctor?" she asked.

"Are you a patient?" he said, recognizing the mother from the Lincoln Continental.

The woman stood in front of the desk. "We're down from Shaker Heights, and well, my husband's having a little difficulty with his, you know?"

"I'm not sure I do."

"His bowels," she said.

Doc Krantz leaned forward with his arms braced on the desk. He felt like putting his head down, right in front of the woman. He could use a good nap.

"I can examine him, if you want."

"That's not exactly what we were thinking." She pulled at her lower lip. "I mean, we're sure you're a good doctor, capable and everything."

"Then just what did you folks have in mind?" he said, irritated.

"We were wondering what he could take. You know, something he could get here in town. A prescription, perhaps." The words leapt from her mouth, each spoken faster than the last. "I mean, just till we can see our own doctor. Not that you're not qualified but, you know how it is."

Doc Krantz looked at his desk. He picked up a pen and scrawled across his prescription pad: *Broad Run Dairy. ½ pound of aged Swiss.* He tore off the page and handed it to the woman.

"This place will have what you need."

Her brow pleated. "I don't understand."

"Cheese, Madame, that's the ticket here. Have him eat a wedge of Ivan's cheese. That'll clog his pipes better than any medicine I know."

The woman stormed from the room.

Doc Krantz watched her through the window. She crossed the street and yanked open the door of Shumacher's General Store. The doctor spun in his chair. He studied his medical license on the wall, recalling the first day of his practice with a vividness that startled him. He remembered in detail the drive out to the Bolten farm, finding Troy's son in the wheat, legs mangled by the combine. The boy had died ten minutes later. Doc Krantz still could picture the young man's face: how he'd looked so peaceful as his life flowed away, eyes toward heaven as if searching for angels.

He'd treated many such cases over the years. Tractors had overturned, crushing farmers under the big wheels, men had caught their hands in the field mowers and bled to death before reaching the house. Then there was the Cort boy. Riding on top of the hay wagon, he caught his head between the barn and the tightly packed bales.

Doc Krantz frowned. He treated routine bowel problems as much as farming accidents anymore. The world had altered right before his eyes, becoming something as foreign as that park in Orlando.

The telephone rang on his desk. It was probably Shumacher, calling to scold him for picking on the tourists again. He sighed and reached for the receiver.

Erban stood in the corner of the room, watching the doctor unpack his bag. He recalled the last time Doc Krantz had come to the farm, many years ago. His parents had been so sick. Erban stuffed his hands into his pockets. He wondered what Harlan would say when he got home.

Doc Krantz pushed his glasses higher onto his nose. He counted the seconds off with his watch, holding Elizabeth's wrist between his fingers. "Ninety-eight," he grumbled. He pulled the thermometer from her mouth, shook it in obvious disgust. "A hundred and three degrees." The doctor turned to Erban. "How long has she been this way?"

"A week today." Erban leaned forward. "Harlan said she'd be fine."

"Is your brother a doctor?"

"No," Erban said. "He ain't."

Doc Krantz held a stethoscope against her chest. Elizabeth whimpered at his touch. "I can't understand what you boys were thinking. Don't you even believe in medical care anymore?"

"My brother thought she was faking it."

"Your brother thought wrong."

Erban nodded. He stared out the window at the fallow patch of garden. The wind had dragged the last of the leaves from the trees, where they lay a foot deep across the ground. Soon would come the snow that would cover the ground till spring.

When Harlan returned from town, Doc Krantz met him at the door. Erban peeked around the doctor's shoulder.

"She's a sick woman," Doc Krantz said. "As bad a case of mono as I've seen. She's got pneumonia as well."

Harlan shot Erban a hard look. "I thought I told you to leave this be?"

"Now, Harlan," Doc Krantz said, "don't you start on your brother. He did the right thing here."

A frown clouded Harlan's features.

"And I'll tell you one thing," the doctor continued, "it's cold enough in that bedroom to keep milk from spoiling. I think a few days at the hospital would do this woman a world of good."

Harlan stomped his foot on the floor. "No hospitals," he shouted. "None of my money for fever and chills."

Standing in the corner beside the couch, Erban wished he could disappear. He wondered if he'd made the right decision, calling the doctor the way he did. Maybe he should have let the whole thing be.

"Tell me how much we owe," he said.

Doc Krantz leveled his steady gaze at Erban. "You know I couldn't have saved your mother and father. They called me out here much too late. But this is different. She needs medical attention." The doctor continued to stare. "We have to do something."

"That woman's only forty years old," Harlan said abruptly, surprising them. He laughed as if that fact had settled everything. "She's as strong as a mule."

The doctor shook his fist in the air. "Don't you understand she could die?" His face turned bright scarlet. "Let me get her into town."

"You come near my wife and you'll answer to me," Harlan said. He stamped to his bedroom and slammed the door.

"Something must be done, Erban. She can't go on with this kind of treatment." Doc Krantz opened his leather bag and pulled out a bottle. "Give her two of these every four hours. I'll bring out a full prescription tomorrow. We'll do our best to take care of her right here." He shook his head. "I hope it's enough."

"Will she be all right?"

"I wish I could answer that." Doc Krantz gathered his coat

from off the couch. "She needs to be fed every few hours, lots of soups and liquids. She needs to be kept warm."

"I'll do my best."

The doctor put on his hat. "You'll have to do more than that. Her condition depends on you. I'll come first thing in the morning."

Erban listened to the doctor's Buick rumble off into the night. The moths roamed his stomach, wings beating rapidly. He looked down the hall at the closed door.

An idea took shape.

With great effort, Erban dragged the bed from his room. He pushed it close to the wood stove. Next he shoved the couch onto the porch. From the closet he brought out his mother's prize quilts and piled them on the bed. Both legs twitched with fear. What he was about to do was crazy, but had to be done.

He walked into his brother's room.

Harlan lay snoring on his back. Erban hesitated a moment, confused. His stomach churned so much he thought he might be sick. He didn't know what Harlan would do if he woke up and found Lizzy gone.

Erban knelt beside the bed on Elizabeth's side. He slid his arms under her wide back, careful not to shake the mattress. Her nightgown soaked his shirt. He tried to lift her and couldn't. Erban thought quickly. He pulled Elizabeth to the edge of the bed and crouched down. On a silent count of three he rolled her over and lifted with his legs, staggering into the dresser. After a moment he found his balance. He gulped air. He weaved his way slowly across the creaking floor.

At the door her head bumped the frame. Her knees wedged against the other side. For a brief second he feared she wouldn't fit through. His back began to spasm, shooting a hot line of pain down his legs. He didn't have much time. Erban lowered his head and charged forward, squeezing her body into the kitchen.

At last he dropped Elizabeth onto his bed. The momentum pulled him down onto her, the springs protesting loudly as if to collapse. His head knocked against her chest. Pushing away, he found his hands on her breasts. He scrambled to his feet. He wrestled with the covers and sat down, breathing in wrenching heaves.

During the night, Erban stoked the fire and kept the quilts pulled to her chin. Elizabeth lay in a feverish sleep. Each time she turned over she moaned. She seemed like a different woman. He studied the curved lines of her face. He wondered how Harlan felt with that great softness smothering him. How it must be to hold her close. Her breasts had been heavy and full under his hands—like nothing he'd ever touched before. In the stillness of the house Erban reached out and rested a fingertip on her shoulder. He pulled his hand back rapidly, as if her hot skin had burned him.

Erban woke to his brother staring him in the face. He jumped in the chair, hands raised.

"What's all this?" Harlan growled through clenched teeth. "You stealing my wife?"

Erban leaned back. "No," he said. "Ain't."

"Then what's all this?"

"Doc Krantz said we'd bury her if I didn't. Like our mom and dad."

Harlan closed his hands around Erban's throat. "Doc Krantz don't know his ass from a hole in the ground."

"What if he's right?" Erban gasped. Spots danced before his eyes. His brother was going to kill him right in the kitchen.

Harlan stared across the room. His expression changed, as if he saw something he liked. He let go of Erban and stood up.

"She's your trouble," he said. "You want to be a faggoty nurse, you do it. It's a pain in my ass anyway." He jabbed a hard finger into Erban's chest. "Just keep your hands off her, hear?"

Erban watched him disappear out the front door.

———————

Elizabeth woke late in the day and looked around the kitchen. She raised her head from the damp pillow.

"What?" she said.

Erban turned from the stove. "You're awake." He lifted a pan from the burner and poured something into a bowl. "I heated some Campbell's."

"Are we alone?" The harsh sunlight through the window stung her eyes.

"Harlan's on the porch. We got the couch out there now." His eyebrows raised. "Ready for some food?"

"Is this your bed?"

Erban put the bowl on a tray. He walked over with his tongue stuck between his lips and set the tray on the table. "I moved it here last night."

Elizabeth struggled to push herself upright. The room spun, then righted itself. "Where did *you* sleep?" she asked.

"In the chair." Erban threw a towel across her lap and brought over the tray. "I kept the fire going."

"What about Harlan?" It seemed too strange to be true. She couldn't imagine the bastard allowing her to sleep one night away from him.

"He knows."

Elizabeth watched Erban work around the kitchen. He washed the dishes and the silverware, wiped the counter. Her head seemed to trap sounds and amplify them. Everything had switched around too quickly to believe. She put the tray aside and closed her eyes.

Harlan and Erban ate supper next to the bed while Elizabeth slept. Darkness closed once again around the farm.

Harlan gestured toward his wife with a spoonful of beans. "Why don't she eat if she needs it so bad?"

"She's weak."

Harlan laughed. "That woman's anything but weak. She's fooled you and Krantz real good."

"We're not fooled neither." Erban looked at his plate. That morning Doc Krantz had examined Elizabeth again. During the visit, he ignored Harlan completely.

"Don't pout, Erban. You just don't know women like I do. They can fool you like anything. Women can make you do things you don't want to."

"But she can't even move."

"She can move all right. It's a trick to get us to go easy on her. Women do this all the time."

"I'm not sure." Erban didn't know what else to say. His brother had always been impossible to argue with. He took a bite of his baloney sandwich. For some reason he recalled the time, years ago, when Hank Slater had stormed into the house. That was the last time Mary had ever come to visit. The two of them had been watching TV when Mary's father hurled open the door and dragged her away. When Harlan returned that afternoon, Erban ran into the yard and told him what had happened. His brother only stared. He carried the groceries into the house without a word.

"What should I do?" Erban had asked. "It's all a mistake. Mary and me were just watching television."

Harlan opened the cupboard doors, storing things wherever he found space. He took a beer out of the refrigerator and sat down.

"Erban," he said. "You're going to have to trust me on this one. Hank Slater did the right thing."

"What do you mean?"

"I mean he saved you a lot of grief. Mary Slater was only after your share of the money. Think about it. She only came out here when I was in town. That should tell you something." Harlan sipped his beer.

"We were just friends."

"Women and men cannot be friends. Any fool knows that. It just ain't possible. They're either after you, or they're off chasing somebody else. They don't waste time hunting with an empty gun." Harlan burped. "I've heard enough stories to know what women are about, Erban. You'd better listen to me on this one." He put his feet on the table. "I know what I'm talking about."

His brother's words crowded around Erban. He couldn't believe they were true. Harlan winked as if there were no doubt in the world he were right. "Do you really think Mary was after me?"

Harlan grinned. "That girl nearly had you roped and tied. You should thank her old man personally for saving your neck." He raised his beer in a toast. "To women and escaping their claws. You're one lucky man."

Now Erban put down the sandwich in his hand. The scrap of memory clung to him, potent, refusing to go away. He looked across the table at his brother, who stuffed a canned peach into his mouth.

"What the hell are you staring at?"

"I was thinking about when we were young."

"Don't think too much, Erban. It'll mess with your head."

Elizabeth moaned from the bed a few feet away. Harlan froze. He looked surprised, as if the dead had spoken from the grave. Under the patchwork quilt, his wife drifted back to sleep.

"Something still on your mind?" Harlan asked, glaring at Erban.

"Not a thing." He pushed his baked beans away from his macaroni and cheese. "I ain't got nothing to say."

Harlan closed his bedroom door with a hard click. Erban waited, then went out to the porch. Wind gusted through the bare branches of the trees. He gathered an armload of firewood, stacking the logs in the kitchen. From his room, he brought out several volumes of the encyclopedia. He placed the books beside the rocker and sat down, wrapping a quilt around his shoulders.

Erban rocked back and forth with an open book in his lap. He felt strangely at peace. The wind rose out of the north, scratching tree limbs against the house. During the night Elizabeth's fever climbed. In no time sweat drenched the sheets. Chills racked her body, tormenting her sleep. Erban watched as haunted dreams flickered across her face. He rocked faster as his worry increased. Beyond the window, the moon crawled above the dark ragged line of trees.

Elizabeth awoke late in the night. She turned to him and smiled. She whispered something he couldn't hear. He brought his ear close to her mouth.

"What?"

"Hold my hand."

Erban wrapped his fingers around her warm hand. It felt like a small fragile bird, a separate living thing.

"That's good."

Erban held her hand for hours, afraid to move. His palm ached. At any moment he expected his brother to rush into the room. The moon rose higher into the purple sky. Erban studied her face in the wash of moonlight. He wished for her to wake again. Maybe she would smile. He wanted something to happen, though he couldn't say what that could be.

When he awoke Elizabeth lay on her side, one hand tucked under her chin. The other hand rested on top of the quilt. Her fingers curled upwards, like a flower that had bloomed during the night.

"It's you," she said, opening her eyes.

He smiled.

"I'm hungry." She glanced down. Her breasts showed clearly under the cloth, the nipples dark and raised. "I'm wet all through."

Erban picked up the bucket by the stove. "I'll get some water." He handed over a nightgown he had taken from her dresser. "Change while I'm gone."

At the pump he shivered against the cold. He resisted the temptation to look through the kitchen window. He worked the frozen handle, watching the bucket slowly fill. He waited several minutes before going inside. Elizabeth sat brushing her hair. Dark circles swept below each eye. Her skin seemed colorless, almost translucent.

"You ready for breakfast?" he asked. "I have some pills for you to take."

"I'm starved." Her arm dropped to the bed as if the brush had suddenly become heavy.

Erban took the oatmeal box from the cupboard and measured the water. While the oats cooked he set a bowl and spoon on the tray. Elizabeth watched him work.

"You're sweet," she whispered. With effort she raised her brush. She moved it through her thick black hair, working out the tangles.

Erban sat with Elizabeth the next night, and the night after that. In the weeks that followed she grew accustomed to sleeping with him at her side. Soon she wouldn't close her eyes unless he was there. Erban spent much of the day in his room. He tried to stay away from Elizabeth and those eyes that followed him wherever he went. It'd been different when he was watching her. That had been okay. But now she watched him with an odd smile on her lips. There was something new about her expression that hadn't been there before. She made Erban want to reduce down to nothing, the way he used to feel when Mary Slater smiled from across the classroom. At times the strange sensation made it difficult to breathe.

To keep busy, Erban tried to rearrange his insulator collection. The pieces of glass and porcelain didn't hold the same magic for him. They seemed somehow dull and uninteresting.

Instead he read about the Great Depression. In the evenings he prepared meals for Harlan and Elizabeth, taking their trays to them. Erban ate with his brother on the porch. Elizabeth ate alone, sitting up in bed.

The first major snow arrived on a Sunday in mid-December. Erban pulled back the curtains and stared off into the darkness beyond the house.

"It's come," he said.

He stood against the porch rail after dinner. Thick flakes sifted from the black sky. Inside the house, Harlan was already in bed. He had gone to his room right after eating. Erban could hear Elizabeth singing while she waited for him to come inside. It seemed like something had been set in motion that could not be stopped. Erban eased down onto the cold sofa. He sat on the porch for a long while, watching the snow pile on the dark shapes in the yard.

6 Sometimes during the day, with no-where to go, Harlan would climb into the truck and putter around the winding back roads, past the Amish farms with their simple houses and barns, looking out the glass, this way and that, like a man searching for something he had lost.

One morning near dawn he awoke with a start. He lay in bed and listened to the stillness of the house. At the window he stood against the frosty pane, looking to where the bare trees of the woods began. The sun tinged the cold sky with color. He pulled on his overalls and went into the kitchen.

Erban slept curled in the chair. He reminded Harlan of the spider monkeys from *National Geographic.* Elizabeth snored heavily, a huge shapeless mound under the covers. Harlan walked between them. Something fierce surged inside him—he felt angry and sick and mean at the same time. He clenched his teeth and stared down at the two figures, opening and closing his trembling hands, breathing hard through his nose. He felt trapped in his own house. He grabbed his coat and keys and ran out to the pickup.

On the road he felt better. The night had brought a foot of

fresh snow, blanketing the fields in white. He turned onto Crooked Run, then turned again onto the new access road to the dragline. The lane twisted behind the other farms, up into the hills. As he drove the sun lost its color. He squinted against the glare of the snow.

Harlan studied the backside of the abandoned buildings. For the first time in years he thought about the people who had lived in them. He remembered walking with his brother to school, the others joining them along the way. Thomas and Ben and Mary Slater. Marvin Hermann. Dave and Sam and Carl Beitzal. They walked the lane in a group, lunch bags in their hands, the smarter ones with a bundle of books, everybody talking about something. Harlan had never once felt comfortable with them. He'd kept his mouth closed the whole time.

He could still hear Marvin Hermann rattle about his cars— how he'd changed the clutch plate the previous night, banged out the dents the evening before that. Marvin was always fixing up some car. He worked on them after supper, staying in the garage until his father ordered him to bed. Harlan glanced down at the Hermann place. The garage where Marvin used to work sat empty, its windows broken. Snow from the drifts blew through the jagged glass.

On the crest of a hill he stopped to watch several deer cross the road. Two bucks led the way, unhurried, followed by three does. Lean and hungry-looking, the herd moved single file, rib cages jutting like metal washboards.

Harlan got out of his truck and moved cautiously toward the deer. One of the bucks turned its head. It studied him, its rack held high and proud, then continued on as slowly as before. The deer drifted into the woods. They moved casually through the trees, stopping here and there to tug at an exposed root. Powdery snow clung to their muzzles when they raised their heads.

Harlan ran with a shout into the woods, scattering the deer.

One of the younger does hesitated, unsure of which way to run. He chased the doe through the trees. Branches whipped at his face. The doe moved left, then rapidly cut right. Harlan leapt over a fallen tree and tumbled head-first at the snow. An expanse of white. Darkness. He panicked and thrust himself upright, brushing the snow from his eyes. Both shins throbbed in extravagant pain. His breath came in gasps, as if the air wouldn't fill his lungs.

The doe was gone.

From the hillside, Harlan looked down on the stripping operation. The dragline sat motionless behind the old Slater place, covered in snow. Heavy equipment surrounded the big shovel, the graders and dozers stopped like large beasts frozen in their tracks. He remembered playing with Erban on the hill when they were kids. Once, they had rolled from the top, turning over and over in the grass, tumbling out of control, laughing, until they reached the bottom. Harlan had loved watching the sky twirl overhead.

Today that was gone: the wild clover, the flowers, the tall green grass. Come spring it would not return, not grow from the clay underneath the cold snow. The wind blew slivers of ice off the trees. Harlan pulled his thin coat around him and turned up the hill to his truck.

When Harlan got home, Erban was sitting on the porch in his coat and hat. Ever since they'd lost the living room—and Elizabeth had taken over the kitchen—the two of them spent much of their time there, bundled to keep warm. Harlan sat listening to the engine tick. He got out and wandered across the junk-filled yard.

"You're out early," Erban said, looking up from his book.

Harlan plopped down on the couch. He still felt cold from his run through the snow. "Lizzy awake?"

Erban shook his head.

"Copperhead's behind the Slater place." Harlan stared off across the bright snow.

"Have they taken the buildings yet?"

Harlan bit his upper lip. His thoughts seemed scattered and mixed together—like the spare parts cluttering the sheds and yard. He glanced over at his brother. Erban leaned forward, wisps of steam escaping from his mouth.

"You ever think about the old man?" Harlan asked. The words surprised him, coming to him, it seemed, from out of the cold air.

"What made you think of him?"

Harlan moved stiffly in the chair, his shins on fire. "I didn't say I was thinking of him. I asked if you ever did." He rubbed his face with his palms. "It's cold."

"Are you all right?" Erban asked. "You don't look so well. Maybe you're getting sick like Lizzy."

"Lizzy ain't sick." He pulled his foil of chew from his pocket and lined his gum with tobacco. "And quit looking at me that way."

"I'll make you some breakfast."

Harlan folded his arms across his chest. For an instant he remembered when they were kids—how he often got angry about something only he understood, sitting for hours in the corner of his room, staring at the wall. Everyone had left him alone when he got like that.

Erban closed his book. "I'll bring it out." He stepped around him and went inside.

That afternoon, Harlan brought back a load of firewood from the mill on Route 21. He piled the logs in a heap behind the house. They were using more wood than usual over the course of the winter. It was because of Elizabeth, the faker. Erban had to keep the place warm for her.

In the burnished winter sun, Harlan chopped wood. He enjoyed the tingle of the ax in his hands. For hours he toiled in the middle of the yard. He wasn't as skilled with the ax as his father had been. Sometimes he hit cleanly, the wood popping with a crack. Other times he smashed into the chopping block. The impact numbed his shoulders in a pleasing way. He swung the ax until sweat drenched his coat. The drops ran freely down his face, falling onto his boots like snow from the eaves.

Harlan dragged himself inside at the end of the day. He lay on his empty bed with his boots still on. He woke in the evening to eat and trudged off again to sleep.

Erban woke mornings to a world of dazzling white. Snow clung to the branches and bare hedges, the thin stretches of the barbed wire fence. The powder lay delicately on the buildings and gate posts, brilliant in the sun. Other times, clouds covered the sky so completely it would be dark at noon. Weeks passed without a hint of snow—days and days of brittle gray skies and deep cold, the ground frozen under the crusted drifts.

Over the months, Erban grew used to sleeping in the rocker. His back gradually sloped forward, conforming to the shape of the chair. Ever since carrying Elizabeth from her room, Erban had not been able to stand straight. He began to use his grandfather's cane to move around the house. He kept it with him always, his gnarled brown hand as if part of the wood.

Elizabeth lay in bed most of the time. She got up only for Erban to change the sheets and help her into clean bedclothes. Doc Krantz made weekly visits to check on her condition. He brought out more medication and consulted with Erban on her care. In time her health improved, allowing her to totter about the room on weakened legs.

Harlan meandered through the day without saying much. He spoke only about the weather, or the price of food at the store. In the kitchen, he ignored the bed as if it weren't even there.

One night in March, with the moon on the snow like liquid

silver, Erban sat watching Elizabeth sleep. It wouldn't be long before she would be healthy enough to return to Harlan's room.

Her face shone in the blue light through the window. She looked peaceful and content, almost happy. Erban wondered if she were dreaming something pleasant. To his surprise she whispered a few words into the room. He pulled his chair closer, leaning forward. Her warm breath touched his cheek.

She opened her eyes.

Erban wanted to move but couldn't. He felt rooted in place, unable to even sit upright. Elizabeth stared without saying a word. She smiled the way she had when he'd taken her hand. In one motion she reached out and pulled him near. Her lips pressed against his own.

He knelt with his knees on the hard floor. Elizabeth gently took his hand. She moved it under her nightgown to her breast, pressing his fingers against the solid lump of nipple. His breath caught. She unbuttoned her gown. Again she drew him close and this time buried his face in her bare chest.

Erban pressed his head into the softness of her breasts. Her hands stroked his hair. Something dark and horrible welled up inside of him, rushing hotly through his veins until he thought he would faint. It seemed about to consume him. He wrenched himself from her arms and rose on unsteady legs.

Elizabeth made no attempt to cover herself. Erban stared at her exposed breasts, then caught himself and shut his eyes.

He opened them again.

"Lay with me." She threw back the covers, patted the bed beside her. She tugged the bottom of her nightgown toward her hips, revealing her thighs. "I need you."

The room felt unbearably hot and close. The floor tilted left and then right. Erban stumbled to the chair for his cane. His shaking hands barely opened the front door. He stood shivering against the porch rail. Icy stars covered the sky. At once he felt small and incidental. Staring at the sky, he imagined the earth as a flicker of light in the blackness of space. He pulled back from the wildness coursing his veins. His chest loosened. After a time he turned for the door. He found Elizabeth asleep.

The next day, Harlan sat on the porch with an old copy of *The Watchtower*. He wet his fingers with his tongue and turned the page.

Erban came out to stand in the bitter air. He looked over the front yard. The rakes and mowers and threshers stood in the snow like an abandoned exhibition of modern sculpture.

"Elizabeth's getting better now," he said. His words made clouds in the air.

Harlan scrunched up his brow. "She wasn't half as sick as she let on and you know it," he said at last.

"That's not true."

"She's not worth it, Erban." Harlan spat into the yard. "Don't get yourself worked up."

"Should I move my bed back into my room?"

"Suit yourself."

Erban shut the door behind him.

One morning during the first week in April, Erban got up early to go to the barn. Dayton Specht had brought over one of his dairy cows the night before, a tan and white Guernsey. The Kerns were to keep it over the summer.

"I'll bring out the feed as well," he had told them. "Some fresh milk'll do you folks good."

Erban picked up the shiny galvanized bucket. With his cane he made his way to the barn. Birds called from the trees, filling the air with bright sound.

Sunlight poured through cracks in the barn. For a moment it seemed as if his father were in the loft, ready to toss hay to the lower barn. Erban pulled up a stool and placed the bucket under the full udder.

"Haven't done this for a while, old girl." He sat a moment, eyes half-closed, remembering the time he learned to milk. His father's hands had encircled his own, demonstrating the exact amount of pressure to use. When Erban continued to milk without help, his dad had hugged him close.

Other memories gathered around him. He recalled the dozens of cats that had once prowled the barn—how they swarmed his feet as he poured milk into their bowl. Gazing across the barn, he expected to see his father run from the empty grain bin, eager to show a newborn kitten. Erban pulled gently on the warm teats. The milk splashed into the bucket with a comforting sound. As the bucket filled he studied his spotted hands.

The door creaked on its rusted hinges. He held onto the teats, listening. The door shut again. Footsteps echoed in the barn.

Elizabeth stood in the middle of the floor. Her dark eyes searched his face. It was the first time they had been alone since she'd moved back into Harlan's room.

"I've missed you," she said.

Erban turned stiffly on his stool. His foot caught the bucket and tipped it. White milk spread toward the gutter, mixing with the tramped-down straw and cow droppings. Elizabeth walked over and touched his shoulder. Her hand rested there until he began to shake.

"You're a good man, Erban. You've got a good heart."

He stared at the overturned bucket.

"Your brother's got no heart. Nothing but a rock there that can't feel."

Erban rose awkwardly and staggered back against a support beam covered with cobwebs.

"I can't."

She took a step forward. "It'll be all right."

He remembered the nights spent in the kitchen. Holding her hand, the kiss. A strange heat ravaged his heart. He took Elizabeth into his arms, pushing his face into the valley between her breasts. Her body crushed against him. It seemed like he was falling, whirling, tumbling down into something bottomless and dark.

Rotten hay spilled onto the floor from a nearby stall. Elizabeth led Erban over by the hand. She nestled into the rank-scented hay, easing him down on top of her. Her mouth covered his. He kissed her in return until he couldn't breathe. He ran a hand along the length of her, delighting in the sensation of her body under his palm. Erban felt her hands at his belt buckle. He released himself to the darkness and pulled desperately at her dress.

Afterward, Elizabeth helped him into his clothes. His back convulsed as if torn apart. He sat against the boards of the stall and watched her dress. She brushed hay from her hair, stepped into her shoes. She seemed a creature of infinite wonder.

He couldn't believe what had happened. He twirled a piece of hay between his fingers. An odd vigor spread through his arms and legs, something he could only describe as the peculiar sensation of being young. It was as if fleeting waves of emotion, youthful and unfettered, passed through his heart and then disappeared.

Elizabeth knelt before him. "Are you all right?" She ran a finger along his cheek and smiled. Erban noticed for the first time that she had been crying.

"What's wrong?" he asked.

The barn door slammed against the wall. Harlan stormed into the room. He stopped short when he spotted them.

"I knew you were up to no good, Lizzy," he yelled.

Elizabeth whirled and charged her husband. She shoved him against the manure spreader. "You're the one who's no good, Harlan Kern."

Harlan shook his head. He pushed away from the spreader, both fists clenched.

Elizabeth stood motionless before him.

"Wait," Erban said, raising his hand. He rose painfully and hobbled in their direction. "Don't."

Harlan swung blindly and missed. He stumbled forward. Elizabeth shoved him again in the chest, sending him reeling against an iron stanchion. He pulled out the leather belt from his pants with trembling hands.

"I'll show you once and for all, Lizzy. I'll bust your ever-loving ass."

Erban leapt onto his brother's back and held on with everything he had. He clung tightly, wrapping his legs around Harlan's waist, digging in. Harlan spun as if the devil himself were on his back. He ran in a crazy broken circle, cut diagonally across the barn.

"Get the hell off me," he screamed.

Erban found a strength he never knew he possessed. He gripped his brother's neck, driving his forearm into the soft part of the throat. Harlan lurched sideways. Off balance, he crashed into an empty stall, breaking through the old boards. Wood flew in every direction. Erban landed on top of Harlan in a pile of moldy straw.

Harlan lay panting under him. Erban climbed off and rested against a broken hay bale.

Elizabeth was gone.

"You're as crazy as a mother fucking loon," Harlan gasped, spitting out a mouthful of straw.

Erban struggled with his breath.

"What in holy hell came over you?" Harlan moved his shoulder and winced. Pain contorted his face. "That woman ain't nothing. Ain't. You should have stayed the goddamn hell away from her."

He left Erban sitting in the corner of the stall.

Harlan blinked at the bright sunlight. He marched straight for the house, kicking at the tall weeds. His shoulder throbbed with every step. The woman had been nothing but trouble from the start. Why on earth he'd needed a wife was beyond him. A man might as well pay someone to beat on his head with a shovel— it was exactly the same thing. He held his arm against his side. What had been going on in his mind? His wife had brought nothing but misery into his life from day one. Take. Take. Take.

And what had she ever given him? Grief. Plain and simple heartache. For three whole years he'd put a roof over her head. And fed her as well. The Lord knew she probably ate her weight in groceries every week.

And how did she treat him in return—chasing after his brother like a bitch in heat? Skinny old ass-backwards Erban. The spider monkey. He should have just invited Satan to the supper table. It was a pitchfork through the heart either way.

Harlan stopped halfway between the house and the barn. He looked from one building to the other. What a total absolute fool he had been to get married. He remembered clearly how it had begun—waking one night in a cold sweat, as if from some terrible dream. A sense of doom weighted his heart. The empty side of the bed had taunted him like an evil spirit lay there, whispering his name.

After that night his loins had burned as if he too were a bitch in heat. He began to stop at the magazine rack at Kroger's, leafing through the girly magazines—whores with their legs open for the camera—and that had only made his pain worse. Then he saw Lizzy's ad in the personals column of the *Cleveland Plain Dealer*. The letter he wrote her ended the peaceful life he had known.

Harlan patted his breast pocket. His tobacco was lost somewhere, probably in the barn. Spitting out a piece of straw, he started for the house.

Inside, the bedroom door was locked. He pounded on the thick wood with the side of his fist.

"Lizzy," he yelled as loud as he could. He hammered on the door again. "You listen to me. Open the goddamn door right this instant or else."

"Or else what?"

The sound of her voice renewed his anger. He reared back and rammed his shoulder against the door. Tears blurred his vision. Pain crackled from the socket to the ends of his fingertips.

Harlan leaned against the door, every curse word he knew hurtling through his mind as if down a dark tunnel. His arm hurt clear to the bone—like some claw had ripped through the muscle and exposed the nerves. He slid down the length of the door. He closed his eyes and waited for the pain to stop.

Elizabeth pressed her ear against the door, not hearing a sound. Harlan was probably scheming right this very minute on a way to get at her. She looked around the room. Her eyes stopped on the oak dresser.

With her back to the wood, she braced her legs and pushed. The dresser didn't budge. She spun around and drove forward with her shoulder, shaking with the effort. The dresser moved a foot. Then several more. Another shove rested it against the door. She wiped sweat from her eyes. The bastard would need a bulldozer to get her now.

Elizabeth whirled. She ran to the window and looked out. Below her, the land sloped down to the garden. It was ten feet from the ground to the window ledge. Harlan would need a ladder for that. She would bash his head with the brass clock if he tried to climb up.

She spotted something in the corner of the room. She stared at it for several moments before understanding what it was. The shotgun. She laughed out loud. *Let him come now,* she thought. *Let him try anything he wants.*

In the barn, Erban finished the milking. He gazed at a piece of straw on the frothy surface of the bucket. The smell of manure wafted from his clothes. His mind was not anywhere near the confines of the dimly lit barn.

My brother's wife.

What would their mother have said? He *was* as crazy as a loon, just like Harlan had told him. As crazy as his grandfather, perhaps. Grandpa Mann had hanged himself in that very loft on a spring morning fifty years ago. Erban imagined the feel of the rope—rough and coarse and ungiving. How had it felt when it closed around his grandfather's neck?

A horsefly shot from the shadows. What would Harlan do, now that he'd caught them? Would he tear the place apart? Would he hurt Elizabeth the way he'd always threatened to do?

Erban jumped from the stool. He picked up the heavy bucket, using his cane for support. Milk sloshed over his shoes. He limped toward the house as fast as he could.

Lunch passed, then supper. Still nothing came from the room. Harlan sat outside the bedroom door. He tried to stay perfectly still. A constant hurt radiated from his shoulder. Any movement rose the demons of pain and their horrible cries.

Several hours ago, Harlan had heard the dresser being moved. He understood what she was doing. He remembered his twelve-gauge shotgun, leaning in the far corner. The box of shells was in the drawer, under his socks and shorts. Elizabeth knew about the shells—like a fool he'd shown the box to her the night she arrived. He had told her never to touch them.

Harlan wondered if she'd actually shoot him, given the chance. He smiled. His wife would blast him to the edge of hell and back.

Erban opened his bedroom door a crack, peeking out. His brother sat cross-legged on the floor. "You okay?" he asked.

Harlan didn't move.

"You want me to fix you something?"

Harlan opened his eyes and glared. He closed them once more.

Near dusk, Erban again opened his door. His brother was still there. Erban eased cautiously into the kitchen. He was afraid to speak. The floorboards squawked as if they would give way at any moment.

He went to the screen door and looked out. Darkness spread out of the east, pushing the remaining light from the sky. He leaned on his cane, profoundly tired.

With Harlan like a statue on the floor, Erban prepared supper. He scrambled several eggs, put toast and butter and jam on the table. He remembered the fresh milk and got out the pitcher. When seated, he called to his brother.

"I made some dinner."

The sound of Harlan's voice startled him. "She's got the shotgun."

"Did you see her?"

"Didn't have to." Harlan rubbed his eyes. "The gun and the shells are in the bedroom." A muscle in his face twitched. "She could kill us in our sleep."

"You're hurt," Erban said, surprised. He stood, but Harlan waved him away.

"Stay right where you are."

Erban didn't move. His brother struggled to his feet, sweat beading across his forehead. He staggered to the door.

"I'm going to sleep on the porch."

Erban finished supper alone. He glanced every few minutes at the bedroom door. Trouble lay beyond the peeling paint, more than he could possibly handle. He thought of knocking to ask if she wanted to eat. He imagined her in the corner with the shotgun on her lap.

Erban washed the dishes and put the uneaten food in the refrigerator. At the window he watched his reflection in the glass—the lined face and worried black eyes, the tuft of hair on top.

He shook his head in disgust.

Erban paced the kitchen long into the night. His cane rapped sternly on the floor. The wood moaned under his weight. Thoughts whirled in his head like something had torn loose and was banging around his mind, lost.

It was all his fault.

What strangeness had overcome him? What evil? Abruptly, as if her image had struggled from his deepest memories, he thought of Mary Slater. He remembered her as a young girl of seventeen: the startling blue eyes, her easy smile, the way her yellow hair caught the sun. She was the only other female friend he had ever known. As he labored across the floor she clung to his thoughts, the smell of her hair again in his nose, that many-scented smell of corn fields and summer rain, freshly mown hay.

All the books he'd studied, as if the answers to his questions lived on those printed pages. Over the years he had read each volume of the Encyclopaedia Britannica. And where had it gotten him? He'd thought if he were smarter—*book-smart,* as his father had put it—then he wouldn't make mistakes, wouldn't do something so horribly wrong. He had been certain he was a wiser man. Plato and Aristotle, the other philosophers whose names he couldn't remember: he had read them all. He hadn't understood every part, but surely he'd gotten something out of all those words. He always felt smarter when he finished a section, whether it was about the noble deeds of some great man, or the earth and its solar system. He had seen in *Life* the pictures of the earth, hanging in space the way a green apple hangs from a tree. The article said men were together in the vast universe. But had that stopped him from doing such a thing to his own brother? Erban smacked the floor with his cane. For all his studies he was no better off than Harlan, who flipped through *The Watchtower* from time to time, and sometimes an old *Reader's Digest.* His brother had never thought another moment about what he read.

"Book learning," Harlan told him once, fumbling around with a bunch of spark plug wires, "will make you into a fool." The wires resembled an overgrown spider in his hand. "Take Doc Krantz and all those books he's read. He's still an idiot." Harlan spat. "Fancy-assed doctors and lawyers and government officials. They put their pants on the same as we do, and some probably need help to do that. Books'll do nothing but constipate your brain. They make it harder to think for the junk crammed in your head." He threw down the wires. "Daddy was wrong about books. They didn't keep him from dying."

Erban had proved Harlan right. Books had not saved him from making a terrible mistake. He had lain with his brother's wife, had plunged into her nakedness until he was spent. What darkness had roared through his mind, driving away all sense of right and wrong?

Near dawn his back began to spasm. He felt as if someone were searing him with a cattle brand. Unable to stand, he went to bed.

Elizabeth sat watching the door, out of sight from the window. The shotgun leaned against the wall. She wanted it close at hand, but not so close as to shoot her toes if she fell asleep.

Near midnight she drifted off, balanced precariously on the narrow chair. She awoke with a start. Beyond the door she heard Erban's cane thump across the kitchen. There were no voices, no other sounds. What had become of Harlan? Did he still wait outside the door, ready to kill her if she ventured out?

She thought dreamily of Erban. They had finally spent their moment together, something she had been certain about since holding his hand. Then Harlan had to ruin everything. How had the bastard known where to look? Only a short time before she'd left him in bed, snoring his raspy death-rattle. It was her bad luck she wasn't able to talk with Erban after they had made love. She had wanted to tell him exactly how she felt. There were so many things she had needed to say.

Erban.

Kind and thoughtful to a fault. That was what she liked about him, the gentle way he'd taken care of her, his infinite patience. A man like that should be nurtured and loved, preserved like a rare flower found in the wild. He had saved her when she was sick, then again this morning with that leap onto Harlan's back. He was truly the only man she had ever met worth knowing.

She woke to pale light outside the window. Her muscles ached from the chair. *I can't spend another day in this room.* Harlan would be sure to find a way to get her. Or maybe he would starve her out. That wouldn't take very long. She remembered how weak she had been the last time he stopped feeding her.

In the back of the closet, Elizabeth found her battered suitcase. She packed the few dresses she owned and tossed in her faded underclothes. Rays of bright crimson soaked the room. She was running out of time. She unloaded the shotgun and returned the shells to their cardboard box. The box fit neatly in her suitcase. From under the mattress she retrieved a wad of bills—money skimmed from Harlan's wallet over the years. She counted almost a hundred dollars.

Elizabeth took a last look around the room. Her heart swelled. At once she felt free and unbridled. Where she would go she had no idea, but that was another matter. Her only thought was to leave and never return.

She snuck to the door and set the suitcase down. The dresser blocked her way. She rammed it aside with her shoulder. She carefully turned the knob and poked out her head.

The kitchen was empty.

Erban's quiet snores drifted from his room. She moved across the floor, holding her breath. Under her feet the rotten boards squeaked like a thousand mice. No matter how she stepped the wood signaled her presence. At last she got to the front door and turned the handle. The hinges grated together. She hurried onto the porch.

Harlan lay on the sofa: mouth open, eyes shut. One arm rested across his chest at an odd angle, tucked like a broken wing. The other arm flopped over the side as if reaching for her.

Why hadn't she heard him snoring? She stared down at his unshaven face. He looked vulnerable lying there. She could do anything she wanted to him. He would never know. She went down the steps and across the yard.

Dew from the grass soaked the hem of her dress. At the truck she stopped and stared. She put down her bag and reached under the hood. It opened with a pop. Elizabeth grabbed a handful of dirty wires and yanked, throwing the bundle into the bushes. She picked up her suitcase and started down the lane.

She hurried away without looking back. The sound of her progress barely disturbed the still morning. The air tasted cool and fresh. Down the road most of the buildings edging the gravel were gone. Above the trees the dragline boom marred the sky. She imagined the shovel tearing into the house at last, lifting Harlan's thrashing body from the ruins.

Behind her she heard a noise. Then the distinctive crunch of gravel. She spun around, the suitcase raised as a shield.

Erban stood ten feet away.

"Where are you going?" He breathed with great difficulty, leaning over his cane. The length of wood looked to be the only thing keeping him upright.

"Are you coming with me?"

He took a labored step. "Where?"

"Anywhere but this cursed stretch of backwoods. There's a world starting right at the end of this lane. We can find a place for the two of us."

"But I don't have any money."

"I've been filching from Harlan for years. I've got enough to last."

Elizabeth put down her suitcase and walked to where Erban stood. He seemed frail in the early light. She took his shoulders and held him at arm's length.

"Your brother tried to kill me. He'll kill you if he gets the chance."

"Harlan wouldn't hurt me."

"What?"

"We're brothers."

"He's full of nothing but hate. How can you live with that forever? You can't let an accident of birth determine the course of your life."

Erban struggled to pull away. Elizabeth let her hands fall to her sides. He took a step backwards, staring down at his feet.

"He's hurt. Who will take care of him?"

"Who would look after you? You can bet it would not be Harlan."

"I need to make sure he's all right. He's the only family I have."

"What about me?"

Erban shook his head. "You will always be my brother's wife. I couldn't live with that."

"But that's not *living* in that house."

"It's the only life I know."

Hot tears stung her eyes. "You were good to me. I won't forget that." She stepped forward and placed a kiss on his rough cheek.

Elizabeth grabbed her suitcase and started down the road. After a hundred yards, she looked back. Erban was still there, dwarfed by the brightening sky. He raised a hand and slowly waved.

She did not return the gesture.

In no time, she came to the end of Willy Slater's Lane. Left lay Sugarcreek. The town would be alive with the clack of Amish buggies, the big auction barn opening its doors. To her right, seven miles away, I-77 stretched like a great serpent, cutting the state in half. She chewed at her bottom lip. Her mind reeled. With a finality that shocked her she started down the road, heading towards the interstate and out of the lives of Harlan and Erban Kern.

"It's separated," the doctor said, frowning. "Not much, but it needs to be reset. I bet it hurts like the dickens."

Erban watched his brother from the corner of the room. Harlan sat at the kitchen table, staring out the window. He hadn't said a word since Doc Krantz arrived.

"Take hold of your brother, Erban. Keep him still."

"How?"

"Lay across him with your weight on his legs. This will only take a minute."

Erban knelt with his chest against Harlan's thighs. One arm encircled his brother's waist. He watched as the doctor probed the injured shoulder. On the armrest, Harlan's knuckles turned white.

"Hold on." Doc Krantz took the arm and tugged. "That did it."

Harlan clamped his mouth shut. Only the smallest sound escaped from between his lips. He looked as if he were about to faint.

"That's all I can do for you," Doc Krantz said. "The remainder is up to nature. You'll need to keep absolutely still in the days to come."

The doctor showed Erban how to make a sling, placing Harlan's arm delicately in the loop of cloth. When he was finished, he stood back and observed his work.

"I'll give you something for the pain."

"Why would I need that?"

"Only a thought, Harlan. Some of us can't tolerate pain. A paper cut makes me feel faint."

"I ain't you."

"That is the God's truth." Doc Krantz placed a bottle of pills on the table. "How'd you do this in the first place? Did you fall somehow?"

Harlan narrowed his eyes. "I bet you were near dying to know. Me and Erban here were fighting over Lizzy. Acting like she was queen of England or something. She ran away this morning." He smiled. "That should keep the townsfolk talking."

Doc Krantz repacked his medical bag. "I'll send a bill," he said coldly. "Pay when you can." He was out the door quickly, rushing to where his Buick sat beside the rusted-out binder. Gravel spun from the tires as he drove away.

"Nosey bastard," Harlan said.

"That wasn't very nice."

"Wasn't trying to be."

"But he came to help."

"That old pecker can take a flying leap. I don't see any reason to humor his ass."

"You've got to start being nice to people." Anger gathered in Erban's chest. "Maybe Lizzy wouldn't have left if you hadn't been so mean."

"Maybe she wouldn't have left if you hadn't poked her in the barn. You tell me who's the angel around here? She probably thought we was going to double team her."

Erban swallowed hard. He hadn't been sure how much Harlan knew. His lungs couldn't get air. He marched for the door.

"Hey, brother."

Erban turned.

"You watch yourself. I just may beat your scrawny ass before it's all said and done."

Erban slammed the door behind him.

Doc Krantz drove fast down Crooked Run. The tires squealed as he took the curves. *That ungrateful fool,* he thought. *The absolute nerve.* He didn't ease back on the gas pedal until he was almost to Sugarcreek.

He turned onto Township 10, away from his office. The road wound beside dozens of Amish farms and newly planted fields. The scene was as peaceful as a man could find: horses pasturing on the new grass, buggies in the drives under broad shade trees. At this time of day, the men would be eating lunch with their families. The sun turned the young corn bright green.

Doc Krantz sensed his anger abating. A drive through the country always relaxed him—it was his personal form of therapy. He reached the intersection with Route 39 and turned right. Ahead the Dutch Valley Restaurant sat perched above the road on a hill. Since the grand opening last summer he had avoided the place, its huge building another example of the Amish selling off the values he so admired. He slowed to a stop. On impulse, he turned into the lot and parked beside a tour bus with *Country Getaway* airbrushed on the side. The lot stretched as wide as the neighboring fields. He stood a moment outside his car, watching the blacktop waver in the heat. With a shrug, he walked to the front entrance.

Cold air met him at the door. The room seemed larger than the parking lot, burdened with scores of maple tables and chairs. Tourists and locals swarmed the salad bar. The whole place had the same constant hum as Harding's Honey Farm.

Doc Krantz waited with his hat in his hands. He felt oddly out of place. A young Amish woman approached with *Hostess* stitched on her dress. She led him to a table near the window and set a menu down. The view from the hill was excellent. He could see far across the gentle swells of earth, the patchwork of farm and field, to the last hill before Sugarcreek. In the distance, the smokestacks of Belden Brick guarded the rolling land. *This place isn't that bad,* he thought. Tasteful and modest, despite its size. The smell of apple pie streamed from the kitchen. He eased back in his chair. Maybe a little change wasn't that harmful.

Doc Krantz ordered the chicken dinner with coffee and pie. The lunchtime crowd packed the room, every table occupied. Waitresses scurried across the hardwood floor, trays of food held high.

A woman spoke near his ear. "Do you remember me?"

Elizabeth Kern stood beside the table. She held his gaze, her eyes guarded. She looked weary, yet happy nevertheless.

"Of course, Mrs. Kern," he said in shock. He stood quickly and offered her a chair.

The woman shook her head. "I have a ride north with some people. I just wanted to thank you for helping me."

"Do you need anything?" He reached instinctively for his wallet.

"I've got money," she said, holding up her hand. She turned toward the exit, then reconsidered. "Erban's a good person. He needs a friend. He deserves better company than that hateful man."

Without another word, she walked away.

Doc Krantz watched her through the plate glass window. She crossed the parking lot and climbed into the back of a white Oldsmobile Cutlass. An elderly couple sat in the front. He noticed the out-of-state plates as the car pulled away. New York. He wished her luck under his breath.

———

Erban returned to his evening walks, but now he moved with his face pointed at his feet, the curve of his back pushed forward, rigid, so he forever seemed to be reaching down to tie his shoes. He often thought of Elizabeth as he searched the grass. He could see her face perfectly if he closed his eyes.

Sometimes he walked too far, and would look up to find himself near Dayton's cattle pens, the animals lowing in the dusky light. Coal trucks roared past as he shuffled home. He held onto his hat in the blast of wind, slivers of coal raining down like sleet.

When he got to the turnoff, the moon would be suspended over the fields, the white steeple of the Crooked Run Church pale in the moonlight.

For weeks Harlan didn't say a word. He sat quietly on the porch with his arm in the sling. He stared down the lane as if he expected Elizabeth to return.

One morning Erban paced around the kitchen, hard pressed to think of something to cook. He opened the icebox as if to find it magically full of food. Inside sat a jar of mayonnaise and a pitcher of milk. No one had gone to town in nearly a month. Since the morning Elizabeth had left, Harlan had barely eaten. He sat playing with his food in a way that made Erban queasy. For the last three days, they ate cereal at every meal. Harlan allowed his to go soggy in the bowl.

Erban glanced into the icebox one more time. The wide empty space stared back at him. He closed the door and went out onto the porch.

"Harlan," he said, clearing his throat.

His brother didn't look up.

"We're going to need some groceries today. We ain't got much food."

"The keys are on top of my dresser."

"You want me to drive?"

"If you're hungry, take the truck and go. I fixed her. She runs."

"But I haven't driven for years. I don't remember how to shift."

"Daddy taught you the same as me."

"But that was years ago. That's not fair."

"Life ain't."

"I can't drive that thing."

Harlan threw down his magazine. "Come on. I'll show you." He raised a hand. "No bitching. It's either this or go hungry. I don't care one way or the other."

"I'll get the keys," Erban said.

For thirty minutes, Erban sat beside his brother in the truck. Harlan explained how to ease forward without stalling, when to shift. Erban listened carefully to the instructions. His head hurt from concentrating too hard. He couldn't get his feet to work properly. He shifted into third and ground the gears. The truck sounded as if it were shredding apart.

"Not that way," Harlan shouted, putting a hand over Erban's and guiding him into gear. "I said right an inch and then straight up. You can't force it. You got to ease her in gently."

Erban practiced from a dead stop. He worked up through the gears and then back down, braking once more. He stalled the truck again. When they reached the end of Willy Slater's Lane, Harlan jumped out.

"Lesson's over." He took out his wallet and handed him a twenty dollar bill. "You remember Kroger's, don't you?"

"You're getting out?"

"She needs gas, too." Harlan slammed the door and started back toward the house.

Erban gripped the gearshift knob with a trembling hand. His left leg shook, barely able to keep in the clutch. He eased up tentatively on the pedal. The pickup hopped forward. Erban pulled hard on the wheel, turning onto Crooked Run. He wrestled to straighten the truck. To his surprise he shifted easily into second. He didn't even grind the gears moving into third.

Erban couldn't believe it—he was driving, on his way to town for the first time in years. He peered over the dash, feeling the wind through the open floor. Under his feet the road streamed in a gray-white blur.

A coal truck appeared on the rise ahead. Erban panicked. The road looked too narrow for them both. He swung toward the ditch and closed his eyes. A turbulent wall of air shook the truck. Erban looked up in time to avoid Floyd May's mailbox. He steered back onto the road. Harlan was right about those coal people. They'll be strip mining hell when Judgment Day comes.

Rich farmland encircled the truck. Erban passed the Warrick place with its winding creek, the willows along the bank fully leaved. Alton Warrick guided the tractor near the fence line, spreading a load of manure. He waved once at the passing truck.

The road climbed next to a stand of pine. The flat green of Machon's Pond tossed off sparks of light through the trees. On the left hundreds of Holsteins surrounded Richardson's Dairy Farm, the animals idle in the heat. The cows formed black and white clusters under every patch of shade.

He spotted the *Welcome to Sugarcreek* sign up ahead. The little shepherd looked friendly. Erban couldn't remember the last time he had been to town. Excitement whipped around his chest. He passed the Belden Brick plant at the edge of town. Flats of rust-colored bricks lined the road, waiting to be shipped. He slowed and turned left onto Main.

The street looked nothing like before. Every single store front had been altered. It seemed magical, as if he had driven by mistake into a European city. Nothing Harlan had said could have prepared him for this: Alpine roofs trimmed in bright red and green, natural wood sidings with shuttered windows, flower boxes overflowing in cascades of color.

Erban rolled down the length of Main, admiring the remodeled buildings. It seemed as good as traveling overseas. Exhaust from the truck clouded the street. The engine sputtered and choked. Along the sidewalk people stopped to stare. Some of them pointed. Erban paid them no mind as he looked around. He continued on toward the grocery store on the other side of town.

Harlan and Erban spent the summer on the porch. They sat at opposite ends of the couch like bookends with nothing between them. Often the memory of Elizabeth Kern hung over them, a vengeful spirit.

One afternoon, Erban stared down the shaded lane as if he heard something coming. The sun threw mottled light on the ground. He turned his head left, then right. He listened intently for something unusual.

From the kitchen came the sound of floorboards breaking through. The rotted wood splintered and cracked. A tremendous crash shook the porch. Erban looked at Harlan as a chain reaction spread throughout the house. Both bedroom floors gave out together. As the foundation weakened, the whole structure tilted to one side. Erban ran into the yard with Harlan close behind. The north side of the house creaked and collapsed in a tumble of wood. Dust billowed upwards. Heavy slate shingles flew off the roof, shattering on the ground.

The wrecked house grew quiet, still, as if losing strength and slowly dying. Harlan looked at the magazine in his hand. He climbed onto the frame of the tractor and settled into the iron seat.

"Better go see Specht," he said.

Erban started the pickup. He sat a moment staring out the windshield. Beams from the house jutted into the sky. Glass sparkled on the ground. Erban sighed.

The house was gone.

At his screen door, Dayton smiled. He shook his head in disbelief. "You boys sure have a time of it."

Erban shrugged.

"I'll get my keys. I think I know what to do."

The bus sat in the middle of the junk yard, bold yellow in the sun. The bright color looked out of place among the faded hulks of the cars. Erban sat between Dayton and his son, wondering what was going on.

"There's your new home," Dayton said, turning off the engine. "What do you think?"

"You mean that bus?"

Dayton waved his hand through the air. "We'll fix it up inside. It'll be as dry and comfortable a place as you've ever seen. Much better than that drafty old house." He climbed from the truck.

"Keep him company, Eddy. I've got to talk to Earl Hayes."

The afternoon waned. The younger Specht watched the cars as if he expected one to come back to life. A hot breeze blew across the lot. Erban turned in the seat.

"You have a family?" he asked.

Eddy looked startled. "I have a wife and a twelve-year-old girl."

"How is it?"

"What do you mean?"

"How is it having a family? I never had one."

The younger man shrugged. "I can't imagine having it any different. For one thing, it keeps you working. You don't have any choice." Eddy turned his hands over and shrugged. His palms resembled untanned leather. Erban stuffed his own hands into his pockets.

Dayton came out of the office. "We got it. They're putting in a little gas for us and starting the engine. I'll drive her out." He handed his son the keys and walked away.

———————

Harlan sat reading the latest issue of *Newsweek* with his back against the shed. His brother had bought it yesterday at the grocery store. Harlan threw the magazine across the yard, disgusted with the world.

A diesel engine labored down the lane. *The coal company,* he thought. *Coming at last with their heavy equipment.* He looked around for his gun. He remembered it was in the basement, under the broken rafters.

A school bus wobbled down the road, its windshield a smear of light from the sun. Harlan waited with a hand over his eyes, watching the bus approach as if it were the angel of death. The wheels stopped on the edge of the grass.

Dayton Specht climbed down the steps. "We'll need to move that tractor frame. Maybe pull some of that other junk out of the way." He pushed up on the brim of his hat.

"What for?"

Dayton winked. "So we can park your brand-new house here."

He laughed and patted Harlan on the back.

Over the next week, Dayton and his sons turned the school bus into a home. Charlie and Eddy removed most of the seats and piled them in the yard. With a torch, Dayton widened the door. He used the tractor to pull the mattresses and wood stove from the basement, along with whatever else could be salvaged. His sons wrestled the stove to the rear of the bus, covering themselves with black soot. They hacked a hole in the roof and pushed the stovepipe through. Dayton sealed the opening with tar.

Erban hung feed sacks over the windows and swept the entire bus. At the door, he unfolded a colorful throw rug from Cora Specht. He stood back and surveyed the scene. It was hard to believe what the Spechts were doing. The bus was transforming into a home. The goodness of their hearts overwhelmed him.

Did this kind of generosity actually exist in the world? His brother had never acted as if it did. The actions of the Spechts seemed to contradict everything Harlan believed. At that moment, Harlan sat leaning against the shed. He glanced up to check on their progress and lowered his head.

"Well, Erban," Dayton said when they had finished, "it looks pretty good to me. I feel like moving in myself."

"What do we owe?"

"You don't have to pay me." Dayton sat his cap squarely on his head. "I was glad to be able to help out. Your father would have done the same thing." He climbed into the pickup with his sons and drove away.

Erban watched the truck melt into the tunnel of trees. Dust sifted back to the ground. From the big oak near the yard the whine of the cicadas rose, then fell.

Harlan stood up and rubbed his eyes. He walked over to Erban, holding his sore arm against his side. He mounted the steps to the bus without speaking. The springs to his bed squeaked under his weight.

Erban looked over at the remains of his house. He felt as if that part of his life were lost, his memories tangled somewhere in the basement with the broken furniture and smashed glass. He recalled the years spent in the living room, watching television with Harlan. The days had passed like an endless dream: reading the encyclopedia, eating meals, listening to his brother complain. His whole life could have been captured in a single week, repeated over and over again.

The old couch hunkered in the weeds near the bus. Erban sat on the familiar cushions. He listened to the scream of the cicadas swell from the trees.

At the end of summer, when the air grew clear and sharp, Cora Specht called her husband onto the front porch. She pointed down to the bottomland below the farm.

"I noticed them a few minutes ago."

Dayton took off his cap. "I don't believe it."

"What are they doing?"

"Helping with the harvest."

In the large field across the road, the Kerns gathered the sheaves of wheat bundled on the ground. They started near the fence line, then worked around in a circle, moving closer to the center on each revolution. The brothers collected several bundles together, then stacked them into tall shocks that stood like an army of giants.

By the end of the day they had finished. Scores of shocks covered the field, each trailing long shadows from the waning sun. Together the Kerns made their way to Willy Slater's Lane, Erban bent-over and moving slowly, Harlan looking straight ahead.

Ohio, 1991

With his cane, Erban poked around the dead ashes in the stove. No sparks, no warm coals. He crumpled a piece of newspaper around some kindling and struck a match. Orange flames leapt upwards. The heat felt pleasant against his cold hands.

Harlan slept on his side, knees drawn inward. Above him, through the broken pane, a gust of wind blew snow into the bus. Erban retrieved the fallen burlap sack and nailed it over the window. At the sound of the hammer, Harlan's eyes snapped open.

"What the hell's going on?"

"I'm here."

"It's colder than a witch's tit." Harlan lifted his head. "It's snowing in here."

Erban rapped the hammer once more. "The fire went out. It'll warm up soon."

"Can't get any colder," Harlan said, dropping his head to the pillow.

The spring storm continued throughout the morning. High winds rocked the bus, its frame creaking. At the windshield,

Erban peered into the whirling snow. Heavy drifts covered the lane, mounding high against the side of the barn. A lone beam jutted through the snow from the wrecked house.

Erban pulled his quilt closer around him. He felt as if he'd been alive forever, an endless stream of seasons passing before his eyes. Around the county, people Erban had known—classmates and neighbors, shopkeepers—fell like withered leaves from the trees. Two winters ago, Dayton Specht died in his sleep. The following summer, Ben Martin had a heart attack while mowing the lawn. The list seemed endless: the Beitzal brothers, Dave and Sam and Carl; Marvin Hermann and Ivan Mueller. His twelfth-grade teacher, Mrs. Hanson, had died on her porch last Easter.

Erban read about the funeral services in the *Times Reporter*. With flowers in hand he went to every one, paying his respects, leaving quietly. Driving home, he marveled how far away his own death seemed.

It felt peculiar—this feeling of permanence, this stubborn idea he'd be around forever. No longer did he suffer the dark pangs of loneliness, that numbing ache that had clung relentlessly to him. Over time his despair had mysteriously slipped away, the way the skin peels from a snake.

For years Erban hadn't crowded his mind with facts and figures from his father's books, knowledge that wouldn't help him live. Looking out the bus window, season after season, he found beauty in the same constant scene. The barn and sheds, the eternal hill—everything etched on his mind from long ago. Yet now he noticed a daily change: variations in the shadows through the trees, a different angle to the crooked fence posts. It seemed every morning brought something new and exciting.

At night Erban stood outside and stared at the cold sky. The stars had a different effect on him now. He didn't feel small and inconsequential anymore. It was as if his spirit had grown larger over time, reaching out toward the sky. Sometimes, standing by the dark hulk of the bus, he imagined his own body threw off light, sparkled like the heavens above.

On the bed behind him, Harlan coughed. "Are you all right?" Erban asked, turning in the seat.

"What time is it?"

"Around five. Are you worse?"

"Worse than what?"

Erban felt his brother's forehead. "You're hotter than the stove. We should get Doc Krantz."

"Cold day in hell." Harlan's face turned dark red. "Old fart ain't coming near me."

Erban sighed. Even if Doc Krantz could make it out, there was nothing to pay him with. What little money he'd made helping Eddy Specht that fall had gone for food.

"Do you want something to eat?" he asked.

Harlan pulled the covers over his head.

The wind howled like a restless spirit looking for a way into the bus. Harlan squeezed his eyes shut, wondering if Satan had finally come. He buried his head under the musty pillow.

In the last ten years, Harlan had never once ventured beyond the mouth of Willy Slater's Lane. After Elizabeth left, a blackness enveloped him, crawling across his tired heart like the branches of a vine. Month after month he wandered around the bus, moving past Erban as if he were a ghost. He ate only what his body demanded, never tasting the food. Clothes hung off him, baggy and loose, as if they belonged to someone else.

One summer day, Harlan roamed the surrounding hills. He stopped on the old access road to catch his breath. Gravel had washed from the wide lane, the ground rutted and collapsing at the shoulder. The Copperhead Coal Company had long since left the area. Before pulling out they reclaimed the land, bulldozing the hills and replacing top soil. They planted rye grass and scores of locust trees. Harlan wiped his brow. The whole area looked different, as unfamiliar as a place he'd never been.

Harlan wandered near the abandoned rock quarry. He kept his head down. He tried to recall the face of his wife, to remember anything about her. He rested on a stone outcropping, breathing hard with his hands on his knees.

Without warning, her image swooped down. Harlan froze. At once he saw her face in great detail: the rough black hair and wide-set eyes, the frown she always wore. She seemed to snarl in his thoughts and become tangled there. No matter what he did he couldn't shake her from his head.

He thought about Elizabeth constantly after that day. He sensed her moving around the bus. When he turned, he saw Erban and no one else. At night he felt the bed springs shift, a heavy weight resting on the other side. When he rolled over the empty mattress rebuked him, sheets and blankets untouched.

Now Harlan sat up in bed, listening. It took him a minute to realize what he heard was the absence of sound. The wind had stopped. He rubbed his sleeve over the window and looked out. Snow fell straight down in thick flakes.

"You're awake." Erban stood beside him in the yellow light from the kerosene lantern.

"The wind."

Erban nodded. "I've heated some Campbell's."

As they ate, Harlan watched the falling snow. "It'll bury us this time," he said, gripping the spoon.

"We'll be all right." Erban blew on his soup. "Eddy'll dig us out."

"What if he forgets?"

Erban touched his sleeve. "He won't forget. Now eat before it gets cold."

They sat in silence for several minutes. Harlan imagined the bus were a coffin under the frozen ground.

"We're going to die this time," he shouted, jumping from his chair. "They won't find us until summer." He towered above Erban, dizzy.

His brother's face remained calm. "Let's finish our dinner."

Harlan hesitated, unsure what to do. He slid into the chair and put his head down.

"We'll be all right," Erban said, his voice as hushed as the falling snow.

The next morning Harlan awoke with a start. Brilliant light filled the bus, stinging his eyes. For a moment he thought he was in a heaven colored in silver. Then he saw the worn quilt thrown across Erban's chair.

Sunlight glinted off the snowbound land. Across the yard his brother drew water from the pump. Powdery snow coated the trees, making the limbs and feathery branches sparkle. Erban's coat was the only dark color for as far as Harlan could see.

His brother carried the bucket across the yard. The deep snow made walking difficult. With his curved back, he looked as if he were about to fall.

"Water pump's not froze," he said when he was close enough. "We can have coffee. Eddy Specht brought the newspaper this morning, plus a basket of food."

Harlan stared down the lane. "I thought I'd died and gone to heaven," he said, touching his chest. The cold air made his lungs ache.

"This is as pretty as heaven, I bet." Erban trudged on toward the bus.

While his brother unpacked the picnic basket, Harlan read the paper. Out of habit he started on the front page and read straight to the end. He read only the first part of the articles, never the continuation on the later pages. If they couldn't say what they wanted to right away, it didn't have to be said. He held the paper at arm's length, leaning back as far as possible.

Only at a distance could his weak eyes focus to read. *The world's going to hell in a handcart,* he thought as he read along. *Everything's ass-backwards and running in reverse.*

A shopping mall had opened in New Philadelphia, near the river. Bigger than a hundred football fields, the paper said, everything you'd ever want to buy, under one roof. Harlan wondered why a person would go to a place like that. People must be crazier than they used to be.

In the television section, Harlan read a story about Howdy-Doody. The museum holding the original puppet had been broken into by vandals. A guard found the doll in pieces on the floor. *They killed Howdy-Doody,* Harlan thought sadly. He remembered watching the show with Erban. Buffalo Bob. Clarabell and her horn. They were probably dead as well. The whole world was dead as far as he was concerned.

On the back page, above the quotes for livestock and grain, an ad caught his eye. He squinted hard at the paper and read:

TONS OF FUN!!!!!!!!
COME AND SEE FIVE FUN LADIES
WHOSE COMBINED WEIGHT EQUALS ONE TON OF
PURE SPINE-TINGLING ENJOYMENT.
SEE THEM DANCE AND SING AND MUCH MUCH
MORE. STAR GRILL 346 FRONT ST.
ONE WEEK ENGAGEMENT. STARTS FRIDAY.
HURRY UP BEFORE THEY'RE GONE!!!!!!!!

Harlan lowered the paper, not sure what he had read. He'd visited the Star Grill, years ago. Then it had been a dark little bar with a jukebox. He had drunk a beer and left. Men and women huddled close, talking low. Their soft laughter had turned his stomach.

This was different—though what it was he had no idea. He read through the advertisement again. A mysterious tingle worked down his spine, the words themselves conveying a separate message, some meaning beyond what was actually there.

Harlan felt a stir in his chest. Something long dormant had awakened inside him. He glanced over to his brother at the stove. With his heart racing, Harlan tore out the ad. He slipped the piece of paper into the front pocket of his shirt.

 Spring returned the following week. Patches of snow lay across the open land, and snow slid in chunks from the roofs of the houses and barns. The melted snow gathered in low fields, sought the swollen creeks and rivers. A raw pungent smell lifted from the thawing ground.

On Friday afternoon Harlan stepped from the bus, clean shaven and dressed in his suit. The truck keys jangled in his hand. His brother stood in the muddy yard, watching a flock of crows wheel overhead.

Erban looked him over. "Going to town?"

Harlan nodded.

"I can get the supplies," Erban said. "I was going tomorrow."

"Ain't going for supplies." Harlan coughed and spat at his feet. "I thought I'd go for a drive. Maybe stop in Dover for a drink." His brother's expression unnerved him. "Can't a man go into town if he wants to?"

"It's been a long time."

Harlan stormed off through the mud. "So what if it has?" He sat a moment behind the steering wheel. The ad rested in his shirt pocket, over his heart. He pushed the clutch as far as it would go and turned the key. The engine sputtered and died. He tapped the gas and tried again. Black smoke billowed as the truck came to life.

Harlan sped down the mud-slick lane, sliding around the corners, fishtailing near the ditch. He drove faster than he wanted to, afraid he might turn around. For the first time in years he thought of his grandfather. The memory sprang forth with a vengeance, as if it had hovered for days below the surface of his thoughts.

One morning when he was seven, Harlan went to call his grandfather for breakfast. He checked the lower barn, then the milk house. He circled around to the hay loft. The heavy door swiveled on its hinges.

Harlan stepped into the darkened room and waited for his eyes to adjust. Manure-caked boots dangled in front of him. From a rope tied to an overhead beam, Grandpa Mann's body turned slowly, as if unsure of which way to look. The head hung at an odd angle. The eyes stared. Around his neck, where the rope bit flesh, the skin darkened to a color as black as a snake. It grew purple toward the whiskered face. Harlan watched his grandfather spin in the air. His own breath stopped. When he got to the house, it took several minutes before he could speak.

The image lingered as Harlan drove the lane. He remembered his grandfather wandering the farm after Grandma's death, looking for something to do. His big hands would flex as he roamed the house, touching anything in reach: the glass paper weights and big leather Bible, the handmade throw pillows on the couch. Mother said he was already dead. When the spirit leaves a person, she told Harlan one night, life ends. She explained people often die in their hearts long before their bodies perish. He found him in the barn a week later.

Harlan shouted and beeped the horn. No one would find him in the hay loft, turning from a rope. He was back among the living. He listened eagerly to each rattle the old truck made. The sounds lifted his heart.

Harlan sat bolt upright. Elizabeth was breathing over his shoulder. He glanced into the rearview mirror. Nothing was there. He looked side to side. The pickup veered toward a gnarled locust tree. He wheeled back onto the lane, never once slowing down.

At Crooked Run, Harlan turned toward the interstate. He mashed the gas pedal to the floor. The truck shook to its frame as it gained speed. He drifted left and over-compensated, edging the ditch on the other side. He thought again of the advertisement over his pounding heart. *See them dance and sing. Hurry up before they're gone.*

The sound of a horn made Harlan look up. The pickup was aimed at a cream-colored station wagon. He pulled back onto his side of the road with a shout. The car honked as it sped past.

Hurry up before they're gone.

On the interstate, Harlan clenched his teeth until they hurt. Constant traffic streamed along his left. Some drivers honked horns, others turned to stare. At last he saw the blue exit sign. Steering onto the off-ramp, he shifted down and pumped the brake. He turned right into town, crossing over the double set of railroad tracks.

Harlan passed the old Bexley Theater. Weathered plywood covered the windows of the building. He remembered going to the movies with his parents, so many years ago. It could have been another lifetime. He parked in front of the bar and gazed through the windshield. *Star Grill* flashed in red, then green. The brightly colored lights reminded him of Christmas.

The room was dark and smoky. He stood at the door, blinking his eyes. Most of the tables were full, the long wooden bar packed with people. A young woman tugged on his sleeve.

"Four-fifty," she said.

Harlan shook his head. "What?"

"Cover charge is four-fifty." The woman patted her hair. "That includes a drink."

Harlan pulled out a wad of bills, the last of the food money his brother had made. He peeled off a five and handed it over. Erban would be mad, but he'd deal with that later. The hostess led him to a seat in the back.

The place seemed bigger than before. All the booths were gone, a new stage lining one end of the room. Several heads turned when Harlan sat down. They looked away when he stared back.

He ordered a Rolling Rock. The buzz of the crowd swarmed around him. For a moment he felt feverish, his head pounding with the surge of his pulse. Maybe Erban had been right about calling Doc Krantz. He seemed to be right so often these days, saying things that appeared wrong but ended up being true.

The room darkened. Beams of light flew about like wild birds, resting on center stage. *Yankee Doodle Dandy* poured from the speakers. Harlan squinted into the whiteness of the lights. From a side door a large woman in black sequined leotards entered the room. Another followed. Then three more. Their outfits sparkled like stars on a winter night. They moved single file to the stage and climbed the steps.

They're beautiful, he thought.

One of the women stepped to the microphone and smiled. Harlan leaned forward in his chair. She had Elizabeth's dark hair and eyes, the same pout to her mouth.

"Welcome to *Tons of Fun,*" she said. "I'm Lou Ann." She waved an arm behind her. "And this is Mary Beth, Robin, Kate and Rosabelle."

Harlan rubbed his eyes. The more he stared at the woman, studied her face, the more she took on his wife's features. *I didn't mean those things, Lizzy.*

Lou Ann pulled the microphone from its stand. She began to

sing, serenading the darkness beyond the stage. Harlan admired her full hips and thighs. The broad width of shoulder. Her breasts strained against the black leotard, as if to burst through. For a brief second she looked straight at him. Harlan gripped his bottle until he feared it would break.

For one hour and fifteen minutes, the women of *Tons of Fun* danced around the stage. They sang songs and told jokes, performed old vaudeville skits. The crowd laughed and cheered. Some threw money onto the stage. In the back, Harlan drank his fifth beer. No sooner did he finish a bottle when the waitress appeared. She took his money so fast he wasn't sure she'd been there.

The room tilted and righted itself. He couldn't tolerate alcohol the way he used to—couldn't tolerate most of life these days. He remembered when he'd been hard as cherry wood. *Now I'm just a sick old man,* he thought. *Weak and helpless as a newborn.* With great care, he raised the beer to his lips. The coldness made his teeth ache.

During intermission, Harlan weaved his way through the tables. At the urinal he peed such a vigorous stream he surprised himself. Beer certainly helped the kidneys. He avoided looking in the mirror on his way out.

A fresh Rolling Rock waited at his table. He plopped down in the seat, exhausted. The room rumbled and shook—more noise than he'd heard in years, crammed into one place. Voices shot from every direction, scattering his thoughts. At the next table, three men argued about the best country song ever written. "Amarillo by Morning" one of them shouted. Harlan held the sweating bottle to his forehead.

In the corner, the jukebox came alive. *I'm yours and you're mine,* it groaned. *Together, baby, we'll do just fine.* A young couple danced near the stage.

Harlan scratched his head. Where had these people come from? The bar hadn't been crowded fifty years ago. People must have kids as fast as they could stand it. The world was cramming itself out of room.

The hostess passed with her tray held high. She threaded through the narrowest of spaces. To Harlan she seemed to glide along, her feet not even touching the ground. She looked younger than he remembered being. He squinted at the clock on the wall. Nine-thirty. It felt more like the middle of the night.

The lights dimmed once again. With their tambourines and ukeleles, *Tons of Fun* took the stage. The entire room applauded at once, the sound of thunder reverberating through the hills. Harlan joined them. He clapped until his hands were numb.

"Thank you," Lou Ann said, smiling over the tables. Harlan stuck his fingers in his mouth and whistled. He was having a good time, by God. He raised his empty beer at the hostess as she sailed past.

Tons of Fun sang in clear bright voices. They strummed ukeleles and played the kazoo. His eyes roamed the stage. Lou Ann belted out a song about love and hearts that stayed true. He tried to sort the words tumbling through his mind. For a moment he saw Elizabeth at the microphone. He clutched at his heart. An emptiness like a great wound bloomed under his chest. *Goddamn it to mothering hell, Lizzy. I never meant for you to go.*

Harlan pressed at the hard plate of his breastbone. He shook his head. Elizabeth had tolerated his constant sour moods and irritabilities. His festering black emotions. She had met each of his rages head on. With Elizabeth, Harlan had felt connected to the world, part of something ageless, unnameable. She had fought to hold him in check, grounding his tormented spirit. Without Elizabeth he might drift off the earth.

He recalled holding her bulk into the night. The heavy weight of her breasts. When she lay on her side her wide hips tented the sheets in a sweeping arch. He had loved the solid feel of her.

For years Harlan had pushed Elizabeth from his mind, refusing to consider what had happened. Now it became suddenly clear, like the countryside when viewed from a hilltop—how you saw at once the contours of the land, its valleys and wooded slopes, the ponds and the flat stretches of field. In one look you knew the completeness of the area. In this way Harlan understood everything: what Elizabeth had wanted, what he had given. He knew, as well, that his life would never be the same.

Harlan downed his beer in one long drink. A cold flush ran through him. Out of nowhere the room seemed full of danger, the stage a smear of colors. *Tons of Fun* locked into focus, blurred again. Harlan gripped the table. He imagined the bar was a ship rolling with the swell.

I'll never make it home.

In a moment the feeling passed. The waitress brought a new beer and took his money in a single motion. Lou Ann sang about how she'd done something her way, though Harlan couldn't make out the lyrics. He rested his elbows on the table, cradling his face with both hands. The conformation of his head—its jutting cheek bones and sharp chin—felt as foreign to him as an absolute stranger's.

As the show ended, Harlan rose to his feet. He shouted for an encore with the rest of the crowd. Tears ran down his face. Soon the women returned, beginning a spirited rendition of *When the Saints Go Marching In*. The whole room sang along. Lou Ann blew kisses at the crowd before leaving the stage.

Harlan sat down in his chair. He waved off the girl when she came for the empty bottle. His stomach had gone sour, as if he might be sick. He studied the star-shaped ashtray on the table. He rose to his feet with a grunt.

People milled around the room. On the stage, *Tons of Fun* gathered their instruments. They turned off amplifiers and disconnected the wires. Lou Ann threw a towel across her broad shoulders.

Harlan stumbled through the maze of tables. Somehow he avoided crashing into anything. He stopped below the stage, watching Lou Ann roll a microphone cord.

She glanced down.

"Do you want an autograph, honey?" she asked. "Or are you just happy to see me?"

Harlan stared at her.

"Do you have anything to write on?"

Something in his mind clicked. He groped through his pockets for the newspaper ad.

"No pen," he said.

Lou Ann smiled. "Wait a sec." After a minute she was back, handing down the torn piece of paper. "I signed it on the side." She winked as Harlan reached out. He stuffed the autograph into his pocket.

"Devil's going to get you for this, honey." She showed white teeth. "I saw you watching us back there. I bet you sinned enough in your mind to last until you die."

Her words came as if through a long tunnel. Heat rose to his cheeks. He staggered back toward a table full of factory men. At the last moment he steered clear and headed for the door.

The night air made him shiver. He looked around a full minute for his truck, then found it in front of him. In the street light, he pulled out the autograph. *Lots of kisses and a ton of fun,* it said. *Love, Lou Ann.* Harlan crammed the paper into his shirt. He dug through his pocket for the keys, closing his fingers around them.

Harlan drove the twisting two-lane with a bottle of Rolling Rock wedged between his legs. The truck wandered over the road. Its headlights lit the mailboxes on one side, the line of fence posts on the other.

An hour earlier, Harlan had stopped at a convenience store on the edge of town. From the window the word *BEER!* cried out in giant red letters. He turned in front of a Greyhound bus and pulled into the lot. *What a country,* he thought. Beer right off the interstate, at your fingertips. He sped down the on-ramp, cutting off a cross-country hauler. He swerved into the fast lane.

Now, Harlan struggled to stay on the road. Crooked Run threaded through the farms, never straightening for long, full of twists and sudden blind curves. He gripped the steering wheel, pumping the accelerator in uneven bursts. Night rushed at the dusty windshield. The scene shifted crazily in front of him— mailboxes and fence posts, houses and barns, cows in the fields. Each loomed in the wash of light and disappeared again.

Harlan swung wide on a turn and grazed a mailbox. He

fought to pull back from the ditch. Fear ripped through him, quick as heat lightning. The tires found the pavement with a loud squeal.

His truck leapt forward as he floored the gas pedal. Through the windshield the road unwound so quickly he cried out, yanking the wheel left and then right. He blew past the Specht house, its windows dark. He passed Willy Slater's Lane without slowing down. The bone-white building of the Crooked Run Church was a ghostly flash. He sped on toward the town of Sugarcreek, nestled ahead in the dark night.

Lou Ann sprang into his thoughts. His brother's image appeared, then faded. He saw his mother and father in their Sunday clothes. He pictured Dayton Specht on his tractor in the field. Mrs. Hanson, Mary Slater, the Beitzal brothers—each paraded through his mind. He felt as if his memory had become unwound, reeling from his head.

Harlan flew over the hill by the old Warrick place. For an instant the tires left the road. He screamed out loud as the truck barreled down the steep backside.

The pickup climbed the rise near Machon's Pond. On the crest of the hill, a sudden flare of headlights blinded him. He jerked the wheel to the right, snapping off a mailbox. As the headlights whipped past, he pulled the wheel hard the other way. In the middle of the road stood Elizabeth Kern. She watched the truck approach, both feet planted on the center line. Her eyes shone against her pale skin.

"God damn you, Lizzy," he shouted, pointing the nose of the truck at her. Elizabeth didn't move. He wrenched the wheel to the right at the last instant. The truck broke the guardrail and shot over the side of the hill, above a grove of pine. The bumper splintered the tops of the trees, pine cones battering the windshield. The pickup sailed over the pond. It landed with a slap on the smooth black surface.

Harlan leaned against the steering wheel. Cold water rose around his feet, moving quickly to his knees and thighs. He tried the door but it was jammed. He grabbed for the window crank. The water reached his waist, then chest, finally covering his head.

The telephone roused Doc Krantz from a fitful sleep. He listened to the shrill ring, then threw back the covers and rose from bed.

By the time he reached Machon's Pond, the truck had been pulled onto the bank. The pickup sat in the early sunlight, water dripping off its sides. Harlan Kern's body lay on the ground under a black tarp.

"Morning, sheriff," Doc Krantz said as he walked up.

Sheriff Dunn touched the brim of his hat. He pulled back the edge of the covering. In the light, the bloated face looked as white as chalk.

"Been in the water most of the night," the sheriff said. "Harry Kinsey saw the truck leave the road around midnight. We couldn't get divers out till dawn."

"I appreciate you calling me first."

"He was a strange one," the sheriff said, pulling the tarp in place.

"He was indeed."

"I never knew what to think of them."

The doctor nodded. "They lived according to their own rules."

"That's one way to see it."

"They never meant no harm to anyone. That seems to be a rarity these days."

"You're right there." The sheriff wiped his brow. "I heard he lived in an old yellow bus."

"*Tuscarawas County Schools* still painted right on the side. I don't see how they made it this long. You'd think it wasn't possible."

"Maybe they knew something we don't."

Doc Krantz looked across the glass surface of the pond. He worked the idea over in his head. "Maybe they did."

Erban sat rocking in his chair beside the bus. He watched the Buick pull into the yard. His stomach tightened as the doctor got out.

"Morning," Doc Krantz said.

"I don't believe I can get up." Erban motioned to the chair next to him. "I've been waiting on my brother."

"That's why I'm here."

Erban gazed down the lane. He didn't want to hear what the doctor had to say. "New leaves are ready."

"Harlan's been in an accident."

Erban planted his cane in the mud and rose. "I've been up all night." He took a step, turned. "Have you ever watched the stars till dawn?"

"I can't say I have," Doc Krantz said, looking puzzled. "Not in a while anyway."

Erban pointed his cane at the sky. "I saw Orion and Auriga. Castor, Polaris and Cassiopeia." He looked over. "I found the Northern Cross."

"I didn't know you studied astronomy."

"My father taught me about it." Erban shuffled forward and stopped. "A hundred million worlds winking from the sky." He hobbled to his chair, suddenly faint.

"How did he pass?"

"The truck left the road at Machon's Pond." Doc Krantz leaned from his chair. "We have to go see him now and take care of things."

Erban looked away. He felt strangely calm, as if he could sit forever, studying the trees and the distant hill. The wind pushed through the leaves and exposed their undersides.

"Let's wait a minute before we go."

Doc Krantz rested his palm on Erban's hand, his touch warm and comforting. "We have time," he said. "There's time."

Doc Krantz arranged for the State of Ohio to bury Harlan Kern. Under a cloudless sky, the plain box was lowered into the ground. The doctor stood next to Erban as Reverend Grey read from the Bible. Off to the left, Eddy Specht waited with his wife.

Doc Krantz drove Erban home after the service. Across the land farmers plowed their fields in even rows, patterns of earth swirling into the distance. The Buick followed an Amish buggy for miles, unable to pass. Doc Krantz saw no need to hurry. The steady clack of hooves sounded pleasant to his ears.

Dappled light covered the final section of Willy Slater's Lane. Above the car the trees formed a thick matted canopy. Doc Krantz parked near the binder and left the engine on.

"We had good weather today," he said.

Erban turned in the seat. "You've been good to my brother and me. I won't forget that, Doctor Krantz."

"Call me Horace." The doctor cut the engine. He didn't want to leave yet, though he wasn't sure why.

"Mind if I come in?"

The bus was cozier than he thought it would be. Most of the seats had been removed, creating an open space that extended to the back. In the rear the wood stove squatted behind two lumpy beds. Homemade shelves holding books and dishes lined the sides. A single kerosene lantern hung from a nail in the bus frame, above a folding card table. Two wooden rocking chairs sat near the front.

"This isn't bad, Erban. I like a simple place."

"It keeps me dry." Erban filled a pan from a water bucket on the floor. He poked around in the stove and tossed in a few pieces of split wood. "The house always leaked when it rained."

Doc Krantz sat on the edge of the bed. "I'm sorry about your brother. It's hard to lose someone."

"To me Harlan left here long ago."

"I've seen that in people myself." The doctor glanced at the junk in the yard. "Do you think you'll stay on?"

"I can't imagine a different place."

"Did you ever think of moving?"

Erban stared out the windshield as if into the past. "Years ago, but I was wrong. This is the place where I intend to die."

"Your father loved this land. I remember him talking about it."

"My father wouldn't like the way it looks. It isn't much the same."

"Could you have done things differently?"

"Maybe someone could have, but not me. My father was able to do things I couldn't. I was never like him."

The doctor leaned forward. "My father was a machinist. A tool and die maker. He never understood why I didn't work in a factory."

"But you did something with your life."

"You haven't?"

Erban paced down the center aisle. "Sometimes I spend hours looking at things I've studied a thousand times before—the trees and the fields, deer on the hill." He stopped. "Have you ever closely watched a thunderstorm? Watched it form in the sky? There comes first a stillness, an absolute silence. Then a sudden change of air. Wind rushes the trees and pulls at your clothes. The storm builds and grows and threatens to burst—it changes every minute. Thunder shakes the hills. Then tingles your toes. At last the rain falls deep into the woods."

"That was amazing, Erban. I haven't heard anyone talk like that in years."

"Neither have I." Erban sat down. "I don't think I've ever talked like that before."

Doc Krantz pointed his finger. "Don't tell me you haven't done anything with your life. That was a wonderful way of telling about a storm."

"It just came out," Erban said.

The doctor spent the entire afternoon in the bus. He drank coffee and shared stories about his boyhood in Pennsylvania. He was amazed at how the workings of Erban's mind closely resembled his own. Here was a man he could talk to, someone who understood exactly what he meant when he spoke of favorite things: the swirling colors of the setting sun, the moon rising over the fields.

"There is nothing like a sunrise," Erban said. "It makes the world seem fresh and new."

The doctor smiled. "There's a moment when you first wake where anything seems possible. As if the day is clean and unmarked, free of the frustrations to come. How I wish that feeling would last longer."

Doc Krantz brought up whatever crossed his mind, however unrelated the topic. He interrupted Erban when something occurred to him, something he couldn't wait to share. He talked about his favorite authors, the men he'd spent his life reading— Dickens and James and Conrad, the works of Mark Twain.

"Conrad was a writer aware of the world," he said. "You'd like him, Erban. He describes the look of the sea when the sun sets and when it comes up, the ocean at rest and in storm, what roams beneath the surface. *Give me a word,* he once said, *and I will change the earth.* Or something like that."

"Do you have his books?"

Doc Krantz thought his heart would burst. "I'll bring out *Heart of Darkness* for you. It's a wonderful book."

Beyond the windows of the bus, the afternoon eased toward dusk. The doctor's voice grew hoarse. He pushed himself to his feet and grabbed his hat. "Find your shoes, Erban. I'm taking you to that Amish restaurant on Route 39. You look like you could use a good meal."

Erban smiled. "I've always wanted to go."

Over the next month, Horace Krantz shared many evenings with his new friend. He spent hours at the bus, talking about ideas and feelings that had been locked away for years. Erban listened with an intensity that continually surprised the doctor, then added some insight to the subject he hadn't even considered.

Sometimes he didn't go into the office for days, turning the appointments over to his new assistant, a serious young doctor named Stone. Willard Stone had recently graduated from medical school, and appeared quite competent, though he spent far too much time with the record books, analyzing accounts, calling in past due bills, comparing overhead costs against the amounts collected from the patients. Doc Krantz secretly smiled when he'd find Stone at his desk with various receipts and ledgers spread around him, looking for all the world like the accountant the older man had never bothered to hire.

One afternoon, Doc Krantz stood at his massive bookcase. He chose one of his favorite books and tucked the volume under his arm. He stopped at the Swiss Hat for an order of take-out, then drove out to the bus.

During lunch, Erban talked about *Heart of Darkness*. Doc Krantz wagged his head in agreement. "You're right," he said. "Marlow was like a witness to the bad things men do. He observed the darkness inside each of us."

The sheriff's car drove the rutted lane. He parked at the edge of the grass and weeds. Erban looked at Doc Krantz and shrugged. The doctor followed him outside.

Sheriff Dunn stood in the yard. "Doctor Krantz," he said, touching the brim of his hat. "Mr. Kern."

"Is something wrong?" the doctor asked.

The sheriff took off his glasses and looked at Erban. "I was just at the courthouse in town. Did you know there will be a tax sale on your land tomorrow?"

"A what?"

"A tax sale. I've been told you owe the county fifteen hundred some dollars in property taxes. You haven't paid anything in years."

"I don't have any money."

The sheriff stared at his boots. "I just wanted to tell you. I wondered if you knew."

"I stopped reading the bills long ago."

"When is this sale?" the doctor asked. He had the peculiar sensation that something valued was slipping away.

"At noon. They'll be auctioning off several properties, this included."

"Can anyone bid?"

"Anyone with the cash."

Doc Krantz turned to Erban. "Why don't I buy the place? I've got more than enough saved."

"What?"

"If I buy it you can stay." The doctor pointed his finger. "I don't want to lose those rocking chairs there. Or that view of that hill."

"But I could never pay you back."

"Look at it as a favor, Erban. Nothing more."

That evening, Doc Krantz drove home with his heart in his throat. He resisted the urge to laugh out loud. His own life, he thought, had as many twists and turns as the plots in his leather-bound novels. He passed the *Welcome to Sugarcreek* sign, cruising alongside the Belden Brick plant and into the heart of town.

For Erban Kern, life felt like a blossom spreading outward toward the sun. His days reflected the newness of spring, full of wonder and a sense of rebirth, as magical as the land greening around him. Leaves bursting forth, flowers blooming in explosions of color—these were the things he held in reverence each dawn.

One morning before breakfast, Erban hiked the hills behind the barn. His cane sank into the ground. He had the impression of having been trapped in some cold dark place. It wasn't only the long winter spent in the bus. The ice and snow. His whole life, he understood, had been covered in a kind of darkness.

On a rounded hilltop, Erban stood blinking at the brightness of the world. He stared in amazement at the budding land. All his life he had admired clouds banked against the sky. The threads of a web covered in dew. He had delighted in the rose-colored dusk, the pastel shades that ran and bled together, separated in new ways. But he had never *understood* these things before. That was the difference. Now these images poured unchecked into his soul—as if he were also full of light, some kind of clean light that awakened his spirit, left him full of an unspeakable truth.

Nearing the barn, he stopped. Two men were waiting in the shade of the oak. A car with out-of-state plates sat next to the binder. He wondered who had come to visit. As he approached, he recognized Fritz Martin.

"Morning," Erban said.

"You look well, Mr. Kern." Fritz took off his hat. "This is my brother, John. He drove all the way here from California."

The man shook hands with Erban. "Do you remember me?" His arms and shoulders were thick and stocky.

"You did the janitor work after class. You were several grades behind my brother and me."

"John's home for Mother's eighty-fifth birthday," Fritz said. "He wanted to see some of the people in the area. Eddy suggested we come and see you."

"I don't get much company, other than Doc Krantz. I'm glad you come."

The Martin brothers sat in the grass, drinking water from chipped cups. Erban leaned forward in his rocker. He had never spoken to anyone who had lived out west. He wished silently more people would come and visit. They could be complete strangers, as long as he could hear about their lives.

"Are the deserts really that big?" he asked. "Thousands of acres of sand and rock?"

"Some deserts are bigger than the whole of Ohio. Hot and dry a place as you'd ever want to be."

"What about the ocean? What color is it?"

John pulled at his lip. "Sometimes it's blue and other times it's green. Sometimes it's both. The color changes with the light."

"Did you ever ride the cable cars in San Francisco?"

"Many times. From the top of the hills you can see the prison."

"Alcatraz?"

"That's the name. But what I really like is the wine country above the city. The hills there are covered in yellow grass, as blond as a woman's hair. It's something to see."

"And Los Angeles? Is there really that many cars?"

"More than you thought existed. The whole city's nothing but mirrored glass and chrome. Everywhere you walk you see your reflection, and not much else. It's not what it's made out to be."

John Martin told one story after another. He paused only to take a sip of water. After a detailed account of a skiing trip to Lake Tahoe, it was time to leave.

"My wife'll be worried," Fritz explained. "We still have work to do for the party." He stood. "You're welcome to come. It's tomorrow at two."

Erban followed them to their car. "I just may do that." He shook hands with Fritz, then John. "I thank you for the stories."

"It was a pleasure, Mr. Kern." John tipped his hat. "Maybe I'll see you at the party."

Erban waved until the car was out of sight. As he turned away, Harlan pushed into his thoughts. To his brother the sight of someone on the lane had meant trouble, the arrival of bad news. To be left alone was the only thing Harlan ever wanted. Now Erban needed people like a starving man needs food. He climbed the bus steps. Horace would be arriving soon for his evening visit. Since buying the farm, the doctor drove out nearly every night. They ate supper together and reflected on the day. Tonight Erban would tell him about California, share what he'd learned.

Erban woke the next morning to sunlight glinting off the windshield. He felt better than he had in years. Though he remained crooked as a locust tree, he wasn't in constant pain. He crawled out of bed as quickly as he could.

With a bucket and soap, Erban stepped from the bus. The morning was warm and clear. Halfway across the wet grass, he realized he'd forgotten his cane. He was walking without it for the first time in ages.

At the pump, Erban worked the iron handle. He filled the bucket halfway and undressed. The breeze nuzzled against his skin. He unwrapped the soap from the washcloth and lathered himself. He scrubbed between his toes and behind his ears, under his arms. When he was clean, he poured the cold water over his head.

Erban looked down at his pale body. Bands of curved rib pressed against his skin, resembling the sides of deer in late winter. Only the barest of muscle held him together. In unlaced shoes he clomped through the yard, the bundled clothes in his arms.

Erban opened a cardboard box near the bed. He unfolded his suit across the mattress, smoothing the wrinkles with the flat of his hand. He was glad Dayton had saved his clothes from the house. Centered at the knee was a hole the size of a quarter. Moths had eaten part of the pocket. He opened the new shirt from Doc Krantz and slid both arms into the sleeves. The material itched at the cuffs and neck. Erban fumbled with the buttons. He snapped his suspenders and pulled the elastic bands in place.

For breakfast, Erban toasted bread over the stove. He held the slice wedged within a bent coat hanger, rotating the metal before it turned red. He sat in the driver's seat and ate while gazing out the windshield. Birds flitted noisily through the trees. A pair of squirrels darted through the web of branches, leaping and climbing as if stillness were something to avoid.

After eating, he opened *Of Human Bondage*. He read a page and set the book down. His excitement, at first a dim stirring in his chest, grew persistently stronger, spreading through his arms and legs. Once more he stared at the birds in the trees. He closed the book and went outside. *It's going to be a special day,* he thought. *I can feel it.*

Erban watched the sun lift higher into the sky. Shadows glided beneath the relics of farm equipment, easing out the other side. He checked the sun's position. One o'clock. He grabbed his cane and started for Crooked Run, moving faster than he thought he could.

Wild flowers colored the banks of the road. Erban passed the stretches of reclaimed land, remembering the way the area had looked in his youth: white two-story houses and red barns, families working outside. Today he did not dwell in the past.

I'm on my way to a party.

As he neared the Martin house, Erban slowed. Dozens of cars filled the driveway. More vehicles surrounded the barns and outbuildings, overflowing into the fields. People covered the lawn at the side of the house. In their dress clothes, the group looked as colorful as a bouquet of flowers. Fritz Martin emerged from the gathering. He waved a hand at Erban.

"I didn't think you'd come."

"Are all these people your relatives?"

"Most are friends and neighbors. There's people here we haven't seen in years. My wife got the idea to bring everyone together." A woman broke from the crowd, smiling as she approached.

"This is my wife, Ariah." Fritz touched her arm. "And this is Erban Kern."

"Fritz has spoken fondly of you." The woman turned to her husband. "The Hermanns just arrived."

"Come," Fritz said. "Let's meet some old friends."

Erban followed the Martins through the crowd. He barely recognized the people who greeted him. He found it easier to identify the children—images of their parents from years before. He nodded at the familiar faces.

"Make yourself at home," Fritz said. "I have to start the ice cream. The food's under the grape arbor." He disappeared into the crowd.

Erban wandered from one group to the next. He wanted to break into the conversations, but wasn't sure how. He stood quietly and listened. From a group near the barn, John Martin pointed and waved.

"Erban," John said, extending his hand. "Got another set of questions for me?"

"I suppose I do."

"This man," John said, addressing the group, "knows about the world. He asked some smart questions yesterday. Liked to have talked my ear off."

Erban looked at the ground. "I'm just interested in things."

"That's the way to be," one of the women said. She turned to John. "I'm going to check on Mom."

"Let's go with her, Erban. This is Martha, my sister."

Erban shook her hand. John rested an arm across Erban's shoulders, guiding him toward the backyard.

"We have Mother sitting in the shade back here."

"I'm sorry about your brother," Martha said as they walked. "I saw it in the paper. It must get lonely out there by yourself."

"Doc Krantz visits most evenings. Eddy Specht brings supplies once a week." Erban smiled at her. "It's not so bad."

Ida Martin sat in a wheelchair near the summer kitchen. She waved a fan in their direction. Her hair looked white as clouds over the blue of her dress.

"There you two are," she said. "I'm roasting out here." John pushed her wheelchair under the eaves, deeper into the shadows. "That's better."

"And who's this young man?"

"This is Erban Kern," Martha said. "From out on Willy Slater's Lane."

Ida studied him through thick glasses. "The insulator man. You must have quite a collection by now."

"I lost them when my house fell in."

"I hope you wasn't in it at the time." Ida pointed with her fan. "Run and get me some lemonade, John."

"I'll go with you," Martha said.

Ida turned again to Erban. "You have a brother, don't you? A grumpy one?"

"He passed away last month."

"My Hans has been dead almost one year."

"I'm sure you miss him."

"To tell the truth," Ida said, looking left and right. "I do and I don't."

"What?"

"Don't get me wrong, young man. I loved my husband, stood beside him my entire life, faithful as a dog." She shook her fan in the air. "But at the same time I was a bit tired of the man. He was a strict one, you know? Rules. Rules. Rules. Rigid as a post."

Ida motioned to come closer. "It's like a breath of fresh air at times. I can sleep as long as I want. Eat when I feel like it. I can even watch the soap operas as much as I please." She lowered her voice. "In some ways, I'm having the time of my life."

"I understand that," he said.

Erban strolled alone through the crowd. He talked with anyone who would listen, eager to hear what events had unfolded in their lives. He enjoyed the stories of families and jobs, of gain and loss and redemption. Here was life in its varied forms, the vastness of its dimensions. The world reflected in the experiences of others.

The afternoon wind started from the fields. Erban stood near the barn, drinking punch from a plastic cup. For miles around the farm the first wheat and corn showed upon the land. The hills across the road were solid green. To his left, a car pulled into the drive. Two women and a man got out, dressed for the party. *Latecomers,* he thought. The three disappeared into the crowd.

Erban crossed the yard and climbed the long set of steps. At the top, he stopped to rest. The porch ran along the front of the house, enclosed with a white railing. Fifteen feet below, Crooked Run edged the building and wound into the distance. He eased into a chair near the door.

The noise of the party rose and fell. A car blew past the house. Then another. With his cane across his lap, Erban closed his eyes.

Sometime later, footfalls echoed on the steps. He sat rubbing his eyes. A woman near his age stood on the landing, wearing a white blouse and skirt. Her silver brooch rivaled the color of her hair.

"Erban?" she asked. In the instant of her voice, he knew. He pushed from his chair.

"You've come," he said.

Mary Slater walked across the porch and lightly touched his sleeve. She smelled of roses in bloom. "It's good to see you, Erban."

"I didn't know you were here."

"We arrived a short while ago. Fritz Martin told me you had come." She laughed softly. "I should have known I'd find you on a porch somewhere."

Erban smiled. Her voice hadn't changed as far as he could tell—still as melodic as the birds, as effortless as the wind. He wanted her to talk forever.

"You look good," he said, offering a chair.

"So do you, Erban Kern."

"Where do you live?"

"We drove up from Marietta. You remember my brother, Ben, don't you?"

"He always dragged his feet when he walked. Is Tom along?"

"Tom died three years ago. I'm here with Ben and his wife."

A truck rushed past on the road below. "And your husband?"

"Passed away ten years this Easter." Mary studied her hands. "Is your wife here?"

"I never had a wife. Harlan passed a month ago."

"Ah, yes," Mary whispered. "Harlan."

Erban let the silence build around them. He listened to the voices in the yard. Someone strummed a guitar, playing the chords to an old country song.

"Harlan spoke to my father about us," Mary said. "He lied to him."

"I know."

"My father wouldn't let me come visit. Harlan had told some terrible lies. He said we were doing things we weren't."

"My brother didn't like us together."

"Why?"

"I'll never know."

Mary recounted the history of her life: the places she had seen, the things she'd done. Her son was in Japan—a country she couldn't imagine—teaching English in Tokyo. "My husband was a carpenter," she said, staring over the fields. "He could make things out of nothing."

Erban talked about his own life. He mentioned the coal company and their digging, the way the land had looked when they were through. He told her about Elizabeth Kern. "Harlan didn't treat her right," he said. "Then he couldn't get along when she was gone."

"Did he love her?" Mary asked.

Erban shrugged.

"It's strange how we live with someone for years, yet never really know them. My husband was the same."

"Harlan was unpredictable as a storm."

"What did you do after the house collapsed?"

"Dayton helped us time and again. Doc Krantz, too."

"There are good people here," Mary said. "I've never found people as good."

"Even when Harlan was mean they never let us down."

The sun deepened in color, slipping down the edge of the sky, above the waiting horizon. Mary touched his arm.

"Let's walk down Willy Slater's Lane. For old time's sake." She held out her hand. "Take this old lady for an evening stroll."

Erban led Mary Slater down the gravel lane. He moved slowly, careful of where he placed his cane. Her hand rested on his arm, holding fast. His heart soared. The years dropped away. He imagined they were seventeen once more, on their way home from school. Ahead their families waited around the supper table.

She leaned against him. "It's been a long time."

Near the edge of the old Slater place, Mary tightened her grip. "Everything's gone," she whispered, looking at him in wonder. "Exactly like you said."

Empty land rested where the house had been. The dozens of tall oaks were gone, replaced with young saplings. Tufts of rye grass spotted the ground. The steep hill that had stood behind the house sloped into a gentle field.

"It doesn't even look the same," she said. "I don't know it a bit."

"But we're still here," Erban said, leaning on his cane. "We still have the way it looked in our heads. We'll always know how it was."

"We also know how it could have been."

She gently took his hand.

At last the sun touched the dark horizon. Colored light soaked the ground. The splashes of orange showed through the black trees and dissolved away. Down the lane fireflies glowed mustard-yellow against the shadows, sparkling like bits of magic dust.

One afternoon a week after the party, the mailman pulled into the yard. Erban hurried to the battered station wagon and peered in the open window. Lyle Kato sat wedged into the front seat, the steering wheel pressed against his stomach. Erban wondered how he managed to steer.

"Got a letter for you," Kato said, rummaging through the leather bag next to him. "Erban Kern, Willy Slater's Lane, Sugarcreek, Ohio." He grinned. "That's you, right?"

"That's me." Erban reached for the light blue envelope as if it were a prize. He hadn't gotten any mail since the property tax bills several months ago.

"It's from a lady friend, I bet." Kato winked. "There's not a man alive with handwriting that pretty." He chuckled as he backed the car away.

Erban opened the envelope. He read:

Dear Erban,

Well, I am home again safely. The house seemed so big and empty when I returned, but that is to be expected.

I received a letter from my son today. He is well. He seems to enjoy living in Japan, though I miss him. He's so far away.

Well, that is all the news I have to report. I had a wonderful time at Ida Martin's birthday. It was good to see you after all those years. You are a good man, still. Take good care.

Blessings,
Mary

Erban folded the letter as carefully as he could, trying not to wrinkle the paper. The past drifted over him: Mary on his porch at seventeen, her hair smelling of leaves and the wind. At times the whole of nature resided within her, everything good and right with the world. He would always have that, the memory of her.

He slipped the envelope into his pocket.

Summer passed as gentle and unhindered as the green waters of the Sugarcreek. The hot sun beat upon the land. In the afternoon thunderstorms raged across the sky, drenching the earth and moving on. Erban watched intently from the bus. He loved the crash of rain on the roof. Brief lines of lightning slit the clouds, leaving jagged imprints upon his eyes.

Late one night in July, Erban heard a car on the lane. The Buick emerged from the darkness. He pulled on his pants and went outside.

"Wake up, there." Doc Krantz opened the trunk of his car. "I got a present."

Erban waited near the door. The kerosene lantern cast a weak light out the bus windows. Doc Krantz lifted something from the trunk and knelt out of sight.

"Just a minute more." He stood and dusted off his pants. From behind the car, he carried a silvery tube with three black legs.

"Isn't she lovely?"

Erban studied the object for a moment. "A telescope," he said, surprised.

"Now you can really watch the sky." The doctor laughed. "Let's find a place to set her up."

"You bought this for me?"

"I thought it might be fun." He glanced around the darkness of the yard. "Let's set her away from the bus."

Erban followed him across the wet grass. The black shapes of the plough and tractor crouched against the night. The doctor stopped. He positioned the tripod in the sand beside the pump. The sky arched overhead, a half-moon nestled in the cluster of stars.

"Sure is a good night for it." Doc Krantz checked the eyepiece. He swung the telescope to the left.

"There she is." He adjusted a knob on the side. "Clear as creek water. Take a look."

The whiteness of the moon consumed the lens. Erban was awed. The silver-colored valleys, the darkly dug craters—it was more fabulous than he had imagined.

"She's beautiful," he said.

"I bought an astronomy chart, too. We can look for the planets."

Erban turned again to the telescope. The universe seemed at once closer, within reach. He stared into the eyepiece, searching for things unknown.

In the middle of the night, Doc Krantz found the red planet of Mars. It reminded him of a lonely king in the void of space. A titan. He turned to where Erban crouched near the water pump.

"So far away," he said. "Makes you feel like we're just specks of dust."

Erban shambled from the pump, the sound of his cane muffled in the sand. He looked into the telescope.

"It makes me feel a part of things. Finding these planets and stars fills me up. I feel special."

"You *are* special," Doc Krantz said, amazed at what Erban came up with. "You're right with how you think." The doctor lowered himself to the ground, stretching onto his back. The indigo sky curved above him.

"Do you ever think of dying, Erban?"

Far off in the woods an owl hooted. "I used to not mind it so much. The thought of it."

"And now?"

"Now I don't even think about it."

"That's good," Doc Krantz said. "I guess I feel the same." He rubbed his eyes.

"There is one thing."

"What's that?"

"I want somebody to find me after I die. Remember when Edgar Ott died? Over in that trailer on Route One?"

Doc Krantz lifted his head. "His daughter found him that afternoon."

"That's true. But nobody checked the barn. When they came months later to empty the place, they found his dog in the barn. A skeleton and a collar chained to a post."

"I didn't know that."

"Sometimes I can't get that dog out of my head. I keep seeing a pile of bones in the straw."

Doc Krantz raised up onto his elbows. He felt as close to Erban as any person he'd ever known. "If I'm still around that won't happen."

Erban eased to the ground beside him.

"You're a good friend, Horace."

The doctor waited until he trusted his voice. "You are, too."

Erban snored in the darkness. Doc Krantz smiled. He looked out at the swarm of stars blowing across the firmament, and closed his eyes.

Doc Krantz awoke out of a dreamless sleep. His bones ached from the hard ground. Inside the bus, Erban was clanking things together.

The red sun advanced above the hill.

The doctor recalled a high school camping trip from years ago. He had woken early the first morning, too excited to sleep. From his sleeping bag he watched the dawn. The sky whitened as light gathered beyond the foothills. Trees shaped themselves from the dark. When the sun spilled across the ground he shouted out loud, waking the other boys. Doc Krantz felt that good now, that carefree. He rose and brushed off his pants. He rubbed the stiffness from his neck.

Erban stood at the stove, frying eggs. "There's coffee ready."

"Do you always get up this early?"

"Some mornings I sleep till noon. Other days I can't wait to get up." Erban lifted the frying pan and slid two eggs onto each plate. He poured coffee from the dented pot. "I could open a can of beans, if you want."

Doc Krantz remembered the conversation from the night before. He was glad they had acknowledged their friendship. Most things between people went unspoken, day after day. All the hours spent with family and friends, people at work. How little of our hearts was ever put into words?

Erban pulled out a chair. "What are you smiling for, Horace?"

"It's nice out here."

"It's quiet, if nothing else."

"Do you ever wish you lived in town?"

"I think about it. It might be fun to have people to talk to."

"It's not that way. Not anymore. Everybody's busy with their own lives. They speed through the day like they can't even stop." Doc Krantz sipped his coffee. "I don't think you'd like living in town."

After breakfast, the doctor eased into his car. Rust covered the fenders and hood, the sides of the doors. "I'll be back tonight. Make the coffee strong."

He played the radio softly as he drove. Dozens of images wandered through his head. He felt on the verge of some important discovery. If he could mine through the clutter, he might find a vein of clear thought. A moment of insight. He'd experienced brief flashes before: fleeting truths that materialized while he did the dishes, or ran water for a bath. But the revelations never lasted. They evaporated as quickly as puffs of steam.

Doc Krantz slowed as he took the curve near the Jenning farm. That odd sensation hung out of reach, lingering on the edges of his mind. He tuned the radio to the local country station and hummed along.

Then, abruptly, the world focused with brilliant clarity. He seemed to have only now opened his eyes. Waves of endless fields and pastures, buildings congregated under the azure sky—every image lucent and precise. In addition to the landscape, the doctor could actually discern the very lives of the farmers. The essence of their being. They made sense to him: their births, their deaths, the moments of experience waged in-between. He even understood the torments of Harlan Kern. The poor fool had just been trying to live.

We all just struggle in the dark.

On the edge of Sugarcreek, the feeling slipped away. In a moment it was gone. The impression left Doc Krantz brimming with joy. He couldn't remember his heart ever being so full. He turned onto Main and accelerated through town.

That afternoon, Doc Krantz sat at the desk in his office. He jotted a note in Mrs. Bloomfield's folder. She had arrived precisely at noon, tormented with yet another bout of arthritis. There was little he could do: the old woman's hands resembled pieces of driftwood, the knuckles and joints swollen and twisted until no

longer human. Painkillers and dietary recommendations, thera-
peutic exercises—nothing worked for long. Only his continued
support and encouragement seemed to help.

The doctor remembered Olan Bloomfield's death. His tractor
had rolled on a muddy hill, crushing him beneath the heavy engine casing. Nothing could be done. Over the years, the five
children scattered across the country. Mrs. Bloomfield finally
moved to town, her days an empty house and cable television.
What good is a family, the doctor thought, *if they are a thousand
miles away?* He scribbled the last of the note and closed the
folder.

Doc Krantz took off his glasses. He still tingled faintly from
the wondrous moment in the car. Willard Stone poked his head
into the office. His assistant looked even more distraught than
usual.

"Are you busy?"

"Just finished, Willard."

Stone moved reluctantly into the room. He closed the door.
"It's a new patient of mine."

"Yes?" Doc Krantz said. Willard Stone was not known for his
way with words.

"She can't pay, sir."

"That happens. Tell her she can send the money in
installments."

Stone stepped closer to the desk. "She says she'll never be able
to pay. She doesn't work."

"How about her husband?"

"She doesn't have one. She has a daughter, though." Stone
tucked both hands into the pockets of his smock, shaping his
mouth into a frown. "She's the one we treated."

"I see." Doc Krantz leaned back and studied his assistant. The
story was growing more interesting by the minute. "And what
was wrong with the girl?"

"Hay fever, sir."

"Hay fever?" Doc Krantz tried not to smile. "Sneezing and watery eyes?"

"They sleep in the fields."

"The fields?"

Stone nodded. "The woman and her daughter don't have a home. They live in the fields."

"Which ones?"

"Sir?"

"Which fields?"

"She says they sleep in different places every night." The young man shook his head. "I'm sorry about this, sir. The whole thing could have been avoided. I should have known better than to bother with them."

"Have a seat, Willard," Doc Krantz said, waving at the chair in front of him. "Let's start again." He watched the man sit down.

"The woman came in yesterday with her daughter. Then again this morning for the girl's follow-up call. When Grace tried to bill her just now, the woman told me exactly what I've just told you."

Doc Krantz leaned forward. "Do you mean she's still here?"

"She's waiting in the outer office."

"Well," the doctor said, "have Grace send her in."

"I don't think you'll have much luck. I've already tried to get her to pay."

"I'm sure you have, Willard." Doc Krantz winked at the man, smiled. "I'll just see what this woman's about. Maybe there's something you've missed."

Mrs. Florence West was an unusual sight. It wasn't that she dressed in men's clothes: a blue cotton work shirt and bib overalls. Or the fact she wore black high-top basketball shoes. What impressed the doctor most was her height—she stood over six feet tall. He noted that she carried her height in a dignified way: no scrunching down to make herself shorter, no bending at the knees.

"Please have a seat, Mrs. West."

The woman sat with her back straight. She appeared to be in her forties, though her skin resembled the color and texture of old shoe leather. Her coal-black hair curved over her shoulder, cascading down the front in a long ponytail streaked with gray.

"Your daughter's name is Virginia?"

"You can't get blood from a turnip. Even a doctor knows that."

"I beg your pardon, Ma'am?"

"I'm not going to pay." The woman showed a silver tooth. "And no one calls me Ma'am."

"Just what should I call you?"

"Flukey. My husband used to call me that."

"And where is your husband now?"

"Dead."

"I'm sorry."

"Don't be. He was hopping a freight train out of town and slipped." The skin around her eyes crinkled. "Are you seeing if I'm available?"

"I was just curious is all." His cheeks burned. He glanced at the folder, hoping to look official. "Doctor Stone says Virginia suffers from hay fever."

"I should have known better than to sleep in the Wilson's barn again. It's dry but the hay stuffs her up."

"So you sleep outside?"

"Mostly in fields and pastures. Sheds or barns if it rains. It's really quite healthy."

"But don't you have a home?"

"I don't know why you are so interested in me, but I'll tell you the same thing I tell the police. My husband left nothing but debts and bad credit. I have no relatives I care to see. Virginia and me travel. We do odd jobs for food and an occasional bus ride."

"You're not from this area, then?"

"My husband was from Missouri. I'm from northern Minnesota, near the Canadian border." The woman leaned forward. "Now that you know my life story, can I go?"

"Where will you sleep tonight?"

"Virginia and me fend for ourselves." She stood, towering above him.

"Wait a second." The words had leapt out of his mouth before he could catch them. He didn't want the woman to leave, though he wasn't sure why. He jumped to his feet.

"I told you I don't have any money. Unless you don't want us to eat tonight?"

He had to think of something fast. "How about doing a little work for me this afternoon in trade? You're not opposed to that, are you?"

"I've done more work in my life than you have in yours." She looked him up and down. "And I'd say you've got about forty some years on me."

"Maybe you and your daughter could do some cleaning— sweep the floors and empty the trash, things like that."

"If I work, it's usually for food. Or a roof over my head. What'll I do about tonight?"

Doc Krantz grabbed the back of his chair to steady himself. *Of course,* he thought. He'd been heading toward this moment since his vision in the car.

"I think we can work that out. I know just the place."

 Flukey West scrunched forward in the seat, trying to keep her head from bumping the roof. Her daughter sat in the back. The doctor turned the Buick onto a gravel road, steering around the ruts where the dirt had washed.

"Where are we going?" Flukey asked.

"A friend lives at the end of this lane."

"Does he know we're coming?"

"He doesn't have a phone."

"Won't he mind us showing up?"

"I got a feeling he won't mind at all."

Her stomach knotted. She had always been careful on the road. Never had she trusted anyone. Now she was in a strange car on her way to God knew where. She would have to keep her guard up. She would have to be ready for anything.

The car rolled through a corridor of trees so thick they blocked the sun. Flukey gazed out the window. Hundreds of saplings covered the hillsides, the land strangely barren away from the lane. Strip mining. If this arrangement didn't work out, there were plenty of places for her and Virginia to sleep.

They could camp this back road for a long time and no one would know.

"This friend of yours must like privacy."

"He doesn't mind company, though."

Flukey glanced at the doctor. The kindness of the old man had surprised her. She'd met generosity on the road, but nothing like this. At first she had thought him senile. Now she didn't know.

In the clearing ahead, an old school bus sat among the weeds. Rusted hulks of farm equipment cluttered the yard. A barn loomed in the trees behind the bus.

"What kind of place is this?"

"A good one," Doc Krantz said, turning off the car. "The main house collapsed ten years ago." He winked at her. "Erban is one of the nicest men you'll ever meet."

Flukey helped her daughter out of the back seat. A bird cawed from the trees. Wind tugged at the weeds around her feet. She walked past the shell of a tractor, avoiding the scrap metal on the ground. To the right lay the mute remains of a house. Poison ivy and other vines crawled over the broken lumber, the weathered wood colorless and pale. Pieces of slate shingles littered the ground.

Flukey saw a man walking toward her. He moved in a curious shuffling gait, leaning on a cane. His dark clothes were threadbare and faded.

Doc Krantz appeared at her side. "He's probably on his evening walk. We can wait in the bus."

"Is that him?"

"That sure enough is."

The man stopped in the crowding dusk. "You brought company, Horace?"

"I did at that." Doc Krantz hurried around to the trunk of his car. "And groceries, too."

Flukey stared at the man: completely bald, bent at the waist, gray-whiskered chin. He could have been one of the hobos that camped near the railroad tracks. She stuck out her hand.

"Flukey West," she said. "And Virginia."

The man had a gentle grip. He seemed harmless as a butterfly. "Erban Kern," he said.

Flukey carried the groceries to the rear of the bus. Virginia sat in one of the rocking chairs, watching out the window. The men erected a card table in the yard. They built a fire to keep mosquitoes away. The doctor hung a new kerosene lantern from the door of the shed.

Flukey fried the steaks and chopped vegetables to boil, opened cans of baked beans. She sweated in the heat. Erban joined her without a word. The two worked smoothly together, not speaking yet knowing what the other needed. She stirred the beans. Virginia would have a good meal coming, a place to stay for the night. What did it matter if the old men were strange? She'd met plenty worse on the road.

They ate in the yard under a rising moon. The kerosene lantern threw patterns of light across the table. The fire crackled nearby. Flukey couldn't remember the last time she had eaten steak. She glanced at her daughter. Virginia concentrated intently on the meal, trying to eat without making a mess.

After dinner, they sat around the fire. Flukey watched flames snarl over the logs. Bursts of sparks lifted into the night and suddenly vanished. From the woods, the discordant pulse of crickets and frogs rose and fell.

"Do you live around here?" Erban asked.

The doctor caught her eye. "Flukey and Virginia are traveling."

"Are you on vacation?"

"Actually," Flukey said, "it's more of an extended holiday."

"Are you staying in town?"

"We wanted to talk with you about that." Doc Krantz cleared his throat. "They need a place to stay tonight. We were wondering if you had room."

"Here?"

"I thought you wouldn't mind."

Erban looked at her from across the fire. "It's not very comfortable, but you're welcome to stay. You saw the two beds in the bus."

"Where will you sleep?"

"Out front here. My back prefers a chair to anything else."

Erban and Doc Krantz discussed at length the upcoming alignment of the stars, poring over a fold-out map of the sky. Virginia fell asleep in the grass. Near midnight, Doc Krantz stretched out his arms. He said goodnight and climbed into his car.

Flukey watched the taillights bobbing into the night. The fire had died to its coals. She stared into the shifting orange glow. Erban touched her sleeve.

"I'll show you where you'll sleep," he said. "You must be tired."

She followed him into the bus, amazed that someone so bent-over could even move. Virginia stood in the doorway, rubbing her eyes. Erban pointed to a rumpled mattress.

"This was my brother's bed," he said. "Virginia can sleep there." He motioned to the other side of the bus, further back. "And that bed is for you. I have some clean sheets in that box."

Flukey stared at the floor. She didn't know what to say. Virginia spoke from the door, surprising her.

"Mom," she said, "I'm sleepy." It was the first she'd spoken the entire evening.

Flukey took her daughter's hand. "Goodnight, Mr. Kern. I thank you for the hospitality."

Erban walked to the front of the bus. He stopped on the steps. "You can call me Erban."

She nodded her head.

Flukey lay awake in the dark. She hadn't slept in a bed in years, the old mattress as soft as pure cotton. Virginia snored peacefully a few feet away. Flukey took a deep breath. The day had swept over them in a mysterious way, from its first dark beginning with that hard-assed Dr. Stone—so moody for such a young man—to the strange old doctor and everything that followed. She raised her head. An owl hooted from the woods. Flukey threw off the quilt and got out of bed.

The yard was awash in silvery moonlight. She found the chairs in front of the bus empty. Across the yard, Erban knelt over something. She worked her way around the farm machinery.

"Erban?"

In the moonlight, she saw him jump.

"I thought you'd be asleep," he said.

"What are you doing?" She looked over his shoulder, curious. A telescope stood aimed at the sky.

"Take a look."

"It's the moon," she whispered.

"Close enough to touch."

"I can't believe people walked there."

He raised his cane to the sky. "Their footprints will never go away."

"Would you go there if you could?"

"I do believe so."

"Me, too."

Erban pointed out the constellations as they wheeled overhead. He made her feel good inside, though she couldn't understand why. She experienced a curious sense of hope in his presence. Maybe it was his peaceful manner. The calm way he spoke. Perhaps it was the contented look in his eyes.

"And this is Venus," Erban said.

Flukey peered through the telescope. "Do you think there are people there?"

"It's a planet much like ours."

"I hope not too much the same."

He shrugged.

"I saw a UFO once," Flukey said, remembering. "Virginia and me were sleeping in a field in Illinois. We watched it for a long time. It hovered over the ground and moved side to side."

"Were you on a camping trip?"

"We usually sleep outside."

Erban stared at her, head tilted.

"We don't have a home," she said.

"You don't live anywhere?"

She resisted an urge to tell him everything at once. "We just don't have a house is all."

"Since when?"

"Seven years."

"You must have seen a lot of places. I bet you've been almost everywhere."

She noted the interest in his voice. It wasn't what she got from other people. Their tone always made her want to run. People acted so superior. When someone did help, they treated her like a stray found in the rain.

"I've seen a lot of places," she said.

Flukey spoke of the towns drifted through. The people of the road. She told Erban about her husband—how the man tormented her with his wandering ways. He had never accepted Virginia, not even at first. Her daughter was born with a slow mind. Mild retardation, the doctors had told her. A lack of oxygen at birth.

"But she's such a nice young woman," Erban said. "She has a wonderful smile."

"Most people don't notice."

"Doesn't she go to school?"

"She did for a while." Flukey tossed a stone into the dark. "She had a special class at the high school. The regular students made fun of her. They teased her in the halls."

"I remember school," he said.

Flukey talked for hours, far into the night. Erban listened quietly as she spoke. He asked a question when he didn't understand, nodded when something became clear. He shared with her stories about his brother, about the years he'd spent with him. The man sounded in some ways like her late husband.

"Harlan fought at things," he said. "He wasn't very happy."

"Did your brother and you get along?"

"I suppose."

"There must have been good times?"

Erban sifted sand through his fingers. "I remember when we were young. Harlan and me hiked to the abandoned rock quarry near here. He spent all day teaching me how to swim. He stayed close beside me in the water, making sure I didn't drown."

"Did you two ever fight?"

"Only once," he said.

Flukey looked through the telescope. She swung the lens through the forest of stars, feeling as if some message lay in one of those distant places. She didn't want to sleep. The night spoke of mystery and promise. If she went to bed, she would wake with the feeling gone.

"Do you ever get lonely?" she asked.

"There was a time when I felt bad inside. The feeling wouldn't stop and it wouldn't get worse. It came mostly at night when I got into bed, a kind of pain like when you are hungry and there's nothing to eat. Sometimes I'd stay awake till morning." He poked his cane at the ground. "Harlan wasn't true company through the years. He worried only about what was on his mind."

"And now?"

"Horace and I talked last evening. Tonight you're here. A person needs others around."

She sat up quickly. "But finding someone you can talk to is like chasing after ghosts."

"That's right."

"What can a person do?"

The wind tossed around the branches of the trees. Erban looked at the rustling leaves. "The trick is to recognize special people when they come along and not let them go. I didn't do that once."

Her breath fled from her lungs. She put a hand to her chest, inhaled sharply. She heard Erban calling to her.

"Are you all right?" he asked.

"Just tired is all."

She got slowly to her feet. Erban took her arm with one hand, holding his cane with the other. His head came only to the level of her chest. He guided her around the junk in the yard.

"Can you make it from here?"

She rested a hand on his shoulder. The sharpness of his bones surprised her.

"Thank you," she said.

Flukey watched him walk away. For the first time in as long as she could remember, she had no worries about the dawn.

Erban woke to the smell of burning wood. Smoke rose vertically from the stove pipe, extending high into the morning air. He rubbed his face with both hands.

"Good morning, Erban." Flukey stood next to his chair. "I thought you were going to sleep till tomorrow. There's coffee on and eggs ready to fry."

She held out his cane. "Let's be washing up now."

Virginia waited in the door of the bus. Her hair was neatly combed, her face scrubbed. She wore a wrinkled dress over her plump body. She looked shyly at her feet.

Inside the bus was rearranged: books neatly stacked, beds made, dishes washed and collected on the shelves. The table was back in place. The floor had been swept from one end to the other.

"You did all this?"

"I couldn't sleep." Flukey pointed the spatula at her daughter. "Virginia, set the table."

The girl seemed more relaxed than the night before. She followed her mother's directions, absorbed with the task at hand. Erban thought the women charged the bus with a certain quality of energy and light.

"What can I do?" he said.

Flukey looked over her shoulder. "Not a thing. It's ready right now."

Erban ate slowly. He glanced up to find Virginia spying on him. She looked quickly away. Flukey watched him as well, though she didn't smile. She seemed more serious this morning. Halfway through the meal, she put down her fork.

"Erban," she said, "I have an offer for you."

"A what?"

"I don't know you really. But I think I do." She bit her lip. "I think Virginia and me would make good company for you."

"What do you mean?"

"We'd like to stay here for a while."

Erban stared at the table top, bewildered. Her suggestion caught him by surprise. He shook his head in wonder.

"This place isn't much of anything."

"My daughter is a hard little worker." Flukey looked him in the eyes. "We can help you out."

"It isn't that."

"She'll be no trouble to you. She'll stay out of your way."

"That's not what I mean."

"Say it then."

"There isn't much here. Why on earth would you want to stay?"

"I'm tired of sleeping in a different place each night. I'm tired of being alone." Flukey squared her shoulders. "We can keep each other company. You said yourself that a person needs someone."

Erban smiled. He felt as if his life were a river changing course, overflowing its banks.

"You don't have to do any work," he said. "You can stay as long as you want."

Her bottom lip trembled. She picked up her fork and slowly began to eat.

Doc Krantz drove out to the Kern place near dusk each day. He brought a different gift each time, something Erban and Flukey needed for the bus. He raided his house searching for items they could use: sheets and pillows, extra dishes and bowls, silverware.

Late one afternoon, he parked in the yard. He sat a moment looking out. The area had been cleared of the rusted farm equipment, the grass and weeds mowed down. The place looked reborn. A canvas tarp hung out from the bus like a porch awning, propped on long poles. Flukey came down the steps, wiping her hands on a towel.

"This place looks as neat as it did fifty years ago," Doc Krantz said.

"Do you like it?"

"You did this yourself?"

"I got the neighbor to help." She waved her hand over the yard. "Eddy Specht brought over his tractor and pulled the junk around back. He even mowed the grass."

"I see you hung those new curtains."

She took him by the arm. "Erban's out picking blackberries. He should be home soon."

Doc Krantz sat in the old rocker. Inside the bus, Flukey made tea. *I've actually made a difference,* he thought. *I've helped someone.* He had often wondered over the years if his existence made any difference whatsoever. Were his patients truly better off because of him? Most of the time he simply prescribed drugs—chemicals that killed the pain until the body could heal itself. When someone was terminally ill there was nothing he could do, other than send the patient down to the hospitals in Columbus, where they suffered before they died. He was helpless when it came right down to it. A caretaker of people while some greater force decided if they lived or died.

But for once he had done something worthwhile. Erban and Flukey were happier because of him. He secretly wondered if his role in their lives had been worked out in advance.

Virginia spoke from beside his chair. "My mother says this is for you."

He took the cup from her. "Tell me how you are."

"I'm fine."

"Do you like it here?"

"Mr. Kern is teaching me to read."

Doc Krantz had to smile. "Are you enjoying it?"

"Not very much. But my mother says I will someday."

Flukey appeared with two more cups. She handed one to her daughter, then sat in the grass. "Stay where you're at," she said, as if reading his thoughts. "I don't mind the ground."

Doc Krantz watched a hawk rise above the wooded hill. The bird pirouetted on the last heat of the day, its feathers the color of wine in the fading light.

"It'll be August in a few more days," he said.

Flukey gazed across the land. "Does it get much hotter around these parts?"

"Humid as the devil in August," Doc Krantz said. "But the thundershowers cool it off."

"I like thunder," Virginia said. "I like to watch the lightning in the sky."

"You and Erban should get along just fine." He held his cup to his lips. "Do you like thunderstorms, Flukey?"

"I won't mind them with a roof over my head." She looked up. "I'm thankful for what you've done."

"It's just some old stuff from my house. Things that I never use."

"I don't mean what you've brought us." Her eyes sparkled like sunlight off a lake. "I mean for bringing us here. I know what you had in mind. I'm grateful."

He tried to act surprised. "I didn't know it would work out like this."

"Whatever you had in mind," Flukey said, "we thank you."

The hawk hovered over the trees. It dropped from sight only to emerge again, rising with one stroke of its wings. The doctor glanced at Flukey.

She's a smart woman, he thought.

Virginia twisted in her chair. "It's Erban." She put down her cup and ran across the yard.

Erban approached from the direction of the barn. He held out the bucket. "I got us some dessert."

"This is quite a home you have," the doctor said.

"Did you hear she got Eddy out here?"

"She's amazing."

"She's done wonders."

Flukey stood up. "I can't take these flowery words." She looked at her daughter. "Let's rinse off the berries, Virginia."

The women strolled to the pump in the failing light. Fireflies flared, then faded. Virginia ran after them, racing from one to another.

"They are very nice people," Erban said.

Doc Krantz nodded. *You are all good people,* he thought, the words running deep into his heart.

It was late when Doc Krantz walked to his car. Over the hills, the stars burned in cold relief. They seemed as familiar as old friends.

At the Buick, he turned and waved. Erban and Flukey stood shrouded in the buttery light from the lantern. The doctor blinked. He thought he saw Flukey take Erban's hand.

The road curved before the car, winding past the blackened fields and pastures. Security lights cast the farmhouses and barns in ghostly hues. Doc Krantz let his thoughts wander. His mind spun with images and ideas. He never could have guessed it would be this way—an old body wrapped around the same young man he'd always been. Inside he still felt twenty-five years old. His ideas had changed, of course, he had learned things about the world, but he was still *himself,* his heart surging with the same strong emotions. He was forever shocked at the old face staring from the mirror. All that wrinkled skin, the sagging muscles: a decaying shell around the bright spirit inside.

A car approached from behind with its headlights on high. It followed closely before pulling around, barreling off into the night.

Hurry, you've got the right idea.

The doctor smiled. He pressed down on the accelerator to feel a hint of speed. A taste of movement. The old Buick leapt forward at once, pinning him against the seat. He gripped the wheel tightly and held his breath.

Crooked Run flew at the windshield. He took the turn at Snyder's Crossing too late, sliding on the loose gravel of the shoulder. On the straightaway he accelerated again. He pulled the wheel too early at the next blind turn. The Buick swung across the center line. The doctor braced for the impact he was sure would come.

The road was empty.

Doc Krantz shot out of the sharp curve. He laughed at his good luck. His Buick climbed the hill near the Warrick place and sped down the other side. He hunched over the wheel. Ahead the road twisted above Machon's Pond, the water through the trees black in the moonlight. He rounded the corner in a blur of speed.

Harlan Kern stood in the path of his headlights.

The doctor rammed on the brakes. Harlan raised both hands, as if warning him to stop. The car fishtailed to the left, then locked into a skid. Doc Krantz closed his eyes. Tires screeched against the pavement. He came to a stop with his front bumper against the guard rail.

His hands were bone-white on the wheel. He opened each finger one at a time. The Buick sat sideways on the road—if someone rounded the corner he would be killed. He backed from the guard rail and pulled quickly away. The pond beyond the trees shone like a pane of dark smoky glass.

Doc Krantz parked in his driveway and got out. He felt as old as the land itself. The street stood in perfect sharpness: the line of parked cars, the trash cans and telephone poles. Mrs. Shumacher's cat sat on her porch, swishing its tail. He fumbled with his key in the lock.

The doctor got ready for bed in the dark. He preferred the shadows over stark light. In bed he rolled onto his back. *You nearly finished yourself tonight,* he thought. *Old fool.* He remembered what Erban had told him. The story of the skeleton chained to a post.

You don't have to worry now, Erban.

He pictured Erban and Flukey standing at the bus, covered in yellow light. He was certain she had taken his hand.

And who will find me?

He closed his eyes. Tiredness swirled over him. *You tried to get me, Harlan.* He pushed further toward sleep. *But you weren't able. Your brother's happy. You can't take that away.* His thoughts flickered.

He sat up in bed.

"I'll show you." He threw back the covers and swung his feet to the floor.

At his desk, he scribbled a note. He would stop at Woodard and Woodard in the morning. Tom would finally write that will for him, something put off for years. The doctor had no living relatives, except ones too distant to matter. A will had never been important until now.

In the dark window pane, his reflection smiled. "I'll take care of you, Erban," he told the glass. "We're two of a kind."

Fifteen miles away, Erban Kern sat with his back against the curve of the rocking chair. Flukey was putting Virginia to bed. He could hear their quiet voices: the sound of water flowing down a brook.

A shaggy line of trees showed on the wooded hill. He smelled rain. Only a few stars were visible, pinpoints of light above darkly massed clouds.

He thought of his brother for the first time in weeks. It was as if Harlan stood outside the ring of lantern light, watching the bus. Erban pictured the constant scowl his brother had always worn. Harlan had struggled at life, he thought, like something you had to growl and grumble your way through, pushing and shoving every inch of the way.

Be at peace, Harlan. Erban peered out into the darkness beyond the yellow light. *Be at peace.*

A breath of wind lifted the leaves, exposing their undersides. The sensation Harlan was near vanished.

He was gone.

Flukey came down the steps. She sat next to him and sighed.

"It's been a good day," she said, more to herself, it seemed, than to him.

Erban remembered how his father always sat on the porch after supper, waiting for Mother. They would sit there as if the night were only for them. He glanced over at Flukey. Her hair poured around her shoulders, a waterfall of silver and black. In one unbroken line, Erban saw his life stretched before him. He felt aware of everything without opinion or judgment.

"Let's stay up a bit longer," he said.

From somewhere in the darkened woods, a hoot owl called once and then stopped. After a minute, it called again. The sound faded. Erban leaned forward in his chair, listening. He tilted his head to the side. He waited for an answer from somewhere on the distant hill.

Cynthia Pauline Wieland

About the Author

Mitch Wieland holds an MFA from the University of Alabama, where he served as fiction editor of *Black Warrior Review*. His stories have appeared in *Northwest Review, Hawaii Review, Sun Dog: The Southeast Review,* and other publications. He grew up near Sugarcreek, Ohio, and now lives in Idaho with his wife, Cyndi, and his sons, Norry and Benjamin. He is currently an assistant professor in creative writing at Boise State University.